ALMOST A HERO

By

James J. Dalton, II
P. J. Renfroe

PENMAN PUBLISHING, INC.

CHATTANOOGA, TENNESSEE

James J. Dalton, II
P. J. Renfroe

ALMOST A HERO

ISBN: 0-9700486-1-0

First Published May 2000
Second Edition October 2000

Penman Publishing, Inc.
4159 Ringgold Road, Suite 104
Chattanooga, Tennessee 37412

Manufactured in the United States of America.

Distributed by Blue Heron Distributors

Dedication

To: All of those men and women who have died in the Armed Services of the United States of America, whether in war or peace – they were all in service to their nation.

To: James J. Dalton, Lt. Col. USA, retired, deceased, my father, and Arline W. Dalton, my mother, very much alive at age 80 – they were my first and best teachers.

— James J. Dalton, II

To: America's warriors: We appreciate the prices you have paid, and the prices you continue to pay, that Americans remain free in a free Republic.

— P. J. Renfroe

Acknowledgements

Without the persistence of Peggy Renfroe and the insistence of Margie Woodhurst this book would never have seen the light of night. Thank you both.

CHAPTER 1

Jack Winston spun his chair around and handed the thick resume across the desk to Mark Douglas. "Hey Chief! Take a look at this applicant."

Leaning forward, his bald head gleaming in the refracted light, Douglas snatched the pages and began scanning the first few paragraphs, his sleepy gray eyes opening wider as he read aloud: "Multiple pilots' licenses, speaks Chinese . . . three Vietnamese dialects, French, Spanish and English. Weapons qualifications include .38 caliber, .45, 9mm, PPK 380, Springfield .03 bolt action, along with AR15, M16, M79, and .50 caliber machine gun—all weapons systems on the Huey and Cobra."

Douglas looked up with raised eyebrows, his mouth open in surprise. "Who the hell is this guy, Jack? James Bond? Says here he has an MBA in finance . . . undergraduate degree from Georgia Tech . . . and an Industrial Engineering Degree, bolstered by highway construction experience. Damn! This sucker even has a law degree and financial experience with the NASD and the New York Stock Exchange . . . helped out in Nicaragua, former Marine, has cooperated with NSA and Secret Service while on advisory status in Washington. His background is Irish/American with a little Welsh . . . and get this—this guy is an American Indian . . . Mohawk, or so he says."

Douglas keyed Jacob Reynolds' Social Security number into the computer and a profile quickly popped up. "One thing for sure, the man isn't lying. Hmmm . . . here's an interesting little tidbit. He's into the IRS for a hundred and seven big ones, as in one hundred and seven thousand dollars — with liens against nearly everything. Looks like some bond swap went bad and he took a deduction in the early eighties that turned sour. Now they're kicking his part-Indian ass."

Douglas punched a few more keys. "Appears to have been a legitimate deduction, but I guess somebody thought otherwise. Could be worth a look — maybe a grudge match or something. I'll have Research look into that to find out if it could have been manipulated."

Douglas continued reading to himself. *Been disbarred for unethical conduct . . . missed a trial where he was to defend a client . . . claimed his office had been rifled and important documents stolen.* Two other clients had brought charges, but Jacob claimed he had never seen these clients, although the paperwork showed otherwise. Betsy Roundside was the State Bar of Georgia's investigator. Douglas had gone to school with her. She had fangs of steel in a mouth that looked like that of a predatory fish. If she was determined to get Jacob Reynolds, then she would. Douglas was aware that she hated men — loved them, but hated them. Probably Reynolds had willingly decided to surrender his license rather than face a public and protracted fight that few had won.

Jacob had spent three tours in Vietnam and was a decorated pilot. Douglas found nothing derogatory in the man's military record, which under the circumstances seemed curious. This did not appear to be the profile of a man who would do something like this to jeopardize his career as an attorney.

"I don't get it . . . something's wrong here," Douglas remarked. "Looks like he did a bang-up job flying choppers for Air America. The man's a stickler for detail . . ."

Mark Douglas leaned back in his chair, still holding the resume, his own experience in Laos spinning swiftly in his head. He thought to himself: *The man is some real son-of-a-bitch.* Douglas vaguely remembered hearing about

Jacob Reynolds in Laos. Only the one called Bulldozer was better—but the Dozer didn't fly. Even so, they had tried to recruit Bulldozer. But of course, he refused, stating that he already had a tank full of deceit.

"So!" Douglas turned back to Jack Winston. "What can we do with Reynolds? He's far too experienced just to forget him . . . but we didn't co-op him, so can we trust him?"

Once again rubbing his hand across his bald head, Douglas continued, "Give George a copy of Jacob Reynolds' resume when he gets back, Jack. But let's leave his profile out of the current update. We may find a need for an outsider for some special job. Send him the usual *thanks but no thanks* letter. We can always change our minds later."

Quietly, Douglas wondered if Jacob Reynolds could be controlled. No doubt the man was extremely well qualified for the agency. Naturally, they could handle the IRS problem, but would Reynolds be too independent in his thinking? He would be learning restricted information, such as he had learned with Air America in Laos, but could he accept these *nationally correct* activities without question, after the deliberate losing battle in Vietnam? Perhaps the man was angry, with a score to settle.

The problem was that Jacob Reynolds did not fit the profile for what was happening to him. The man had proven honest in all his dealings while in the service. So, what had happened? If Jacob Reynolds was in trouble, he was not one to ask for help—he would handle it himself, and that was what worried Mark Douglas.

Douglas pushed his chair back, opened a drawer in his desk and laid the resume on top of the locked box there. He would put it in the system later, after he talked with George.

"Forget the copy, Jack. But send the letter—I'll talk with George or Billy Joe about Jacob Reynolds."

CHAPTER 2

Greedy flames consumed resin rich pellets, heating a spot on the flat top of the old cast iron heater to a deceptively soft pink glow. A Chinese teapot rested its heavy base on the hot spot, spouting steam. Billy Joe Brown wrapped a hot pad around the wire handle and poured boiling water over two teaspoons of instant coffee in a beat up and chipped old war mug.

The call from Jacob Reynolds had disturbed his peaceful morning. He plopped his lean six-foot-four frame down in a blue plaid recliner, cradling the mug of coffee in two scarred but sound, long-fingered hands. He was amazed that he had lived long enough to enjoy this normalcy, this quiet Sunday morning in his private office, his family sleeping in the nearby house. He clicked on the TV to news of disasters around the globe. Needing no reminder of how fragile people's playthings can be when exposed to the elements of nature or man, he turned it off. Putting the mug down on the side table, he pulled his wet-weather poncho liner tighter around him, tucking one corner under his arm, wondering about the sanity of a man coveting a reminder of his warrior days. But wasn't he still a warrior? Albeit one of a matured different sort.

A deep furrow formed between heavy brows as his thoughts replayed the phone call from Jacob Reynolds. "I've found another enemy—or I should say, they've found me," Jacob had said. "They laid out the ground rules and started the game, but they may not know that I invented the rules."

Billy's first reaction had been that *they* had better start praying, because Jacob Reynolds was one wily fighter who, when provoked, did not understand the word *retreat*. He had last seen Reynolds two years ago at a reunion in Chicago for some Vietnam era Marines. When he had arrived, the members of the group were milling around, shaking hands, slapping shoulders and making jokes. Then Billy had spotted Jacob wearing a blue baseball cap inscribed with the words: "We were winning when I left."

Marble Mountain, Da Nang, I-corp, Republic of South Vietnam in the middle sixties had been their first encounter. They had answered the call by John Kennedy: "Ask not what your country can do for you, but what you can do for your country!" *What they'd had by the teeth sure as hell had not been the Peace Corps.*

Billy Joe leaned his head back to rest on the pillow-soft recliner, thinking back to the sixties and remembering that even then Reynolds had possessed the wild factor that only surfaced after his FAC duty at Con Thien. Con Thien was a fire base sitting just south of the DMZ, between North and South, just like the good old 38th Parallel, slightly west of the South China Sea, and an easy target for infiltrating North Vietnamese Army Regulars.

Billy Joe and D.R. had been attached to HMM-265, a medium lift Marine helicopter squadron. Billy Joe would never forget, for he had been the *scared-shitless* newest replacement pilot. Jacob had been one of the guys sent to 265 by what was affectionately called the *fruit basket turnover*. The Marine Corps had as one of its basic tenets something called *unit integrity*. In World War II, Marine units were pulled out of the conflict, reconstructed, retrained and reintroduced into the combat zone with *unit integrity*. Not so in this *little* war in Southeast Asia. Here the leaders, the planners — the *idiots* — came up with their own plan by taking some men from each squadron, switching them to other squadrons so the unit would stay in the combat zone, and the Marine Corps just funneled in replacement pilots who didn't know each other, creating a built-in fragmentation of unit integrity.

Billy shook his head, remembering how young Reynolds had seemed. Still just a kid, he was a Mar-Cad recruited right out of two years of college, then trained to fill the Marines' need for pilot fodder. When they first met, Jacob had been five feet eleven inches of pudgy baby fat, with joy at his edges, alert hazel-green eyes, straw blonde hair and a friendly dimpled smile. These might have been good qualities in the states, but he was sent off within the next two months to Con Thien as a Forward Air Controller, or FAC, meaning the pilot went to a ground unit in a combat zone to control friendly air support.

From the air, Con Thien looked like a flat spider web with a red clay center. All around the edges of the hill were trenches, the Marines' home away from home. Billy remembered flying resupply in on early mornings with food, ammo and water. He shuddered at the remembrance of seeing the lifeless, gray bodies of men caught in the spider web of spiked wire.

Jacob had been at Con Thien for three months when Billy had bumped into him at a coffee hutch by the runway while on a special mission in Phu Bai. Billy would never forget the change from the jovial boy he had known earlier to what Jacob had become. The edge of joy had completely disappeared. Those still alert green eyes wore a haunted look and rested in deep sockets. The easy smile had been replaced by a grim determined set to his mouth. Gaunt, he seemed taller and older, a mere shadow of his former self. Bone thin, long fingers looked like fleshy stiletto icicles. Two pearl-handled revolvers hung from his narrow hips, completing the transformation from innocent boy to formidable warrior.

Sitting on two facing seats in that wooden-floored hootch that smelled of coffee, exhaust, sweat and wet dust pounded up by rain, they had shared the usual jokes, then Jacob had told a quick but revealing little story. As the words unfolded into reality, his soul was briefly exposed. Jacob's eyes were the saddest Billy had ever seen; tired and resigned, yet with a depth of knowing intelligence that Billy knew he had not experienced.

Jacob had begun talking quietly. "I've spent the last three months in a hole dug in the hard red clay at Con Thien. Almost every night the NVA probed our perimeter. One night they came swarming across the wire and many of them got inside the compound. They began dropping into our holes with us and I could hear shouting, struggling and gunfire. Then I heard and felt someone in my hole with me. A flare popped and I saw him clearly, facing me within arms length. His big brown eyes glinted in the flare's light; he was slightly shorter than me, but as they say in the South, he had an attitude adjuster in the form of a large knife in his right hand and he was moving menacingly toward me. My training automatically took over and I disarmed him. Then suddenly I had my hands wrapped around his throat and I began to squeeze with all the power I could muster. His eyes bulged, his arms went limp, but I couldn't stop. He gasped and finally died with my hands still tightly around his neck. Some hero, huh? No sword, no gun, just bare hands, and not even so much as a karate chop."

With a sigh, Jacob covered his face with his hands and shook his head. "Once you've killed a man with your bare hands, there's little anyone can do to cause you *real* harm."

At that point they knew their lives had been rearranged forever. They were on one hell of a "Road Less Traveled," knowing it was not themselves they worried about, but those they loved. They could never explain where they had been, what they had done, which left them in an emotional tangle. The families they had left behind had never experienced war close up, and thankfully, so far they had not experienced the horror. This deceit of emotion to protect the innocent forced them to lead two different emotional lives.

It didn't help that they came from a Christian community and had become warriors, or that it was against everything taught from childhood. That only made the transition emotionally more difficult, but even that was lost in time as reality took over. Even if the warrior wanted to forget the past and be that social, businessman he had become, the past drifted in at the most unexpected times. When a grandchild looked up with trusting eyes, thinking Grandpa was the most wonderful man in the world, hugged and kissed him with such a strong love, he wanted to protect that child forever. Aware that his innocence was so remote from what he had become, he hoped that child never learned the kind of man he really was. The paradox was that if he had not become a warrior, that innocence would not be protected.

Discharged from service, Billy had joined the home-front Marine Corps Reserves, and Jacob had extended for two more tours in Vietnam before the U.S. pulled out leaving the Vietnamese to fight among themselves.

During at least one of those tours, Jacob had flown Cobra gunships; then he had worked for Air America in Laos. That was the worst kept secret in Southeast Asia, a CIA fronted operation to resupply Laotian rebels and only God knew what else. It had changed Reynolds even more. He developed a calm confidence, a jungle cat wariness, controlled, directed and deadly, yet also untamable and unpredictable. Because of his uncanny ability to hone in on the enemy, the *grunts* dubbed him D.R. for *Dead Reckon*.

Billy knew that as friends go, Jacob Reynolds, aka D.R., was a man one could trust. When D.R. had called, Billy knew all hell was about to break loose. His tone had been calm, but Billy imagined the people D.R. was looking for were the most deadly warriors in their deadly business. Billy had given D.R. the requested numbers, knowing that whoever was after him would deserve whatever they got. D.R. would not do anything foolish. The man had never left a Marine behind—dead or alive—when he departed a combat situation. He always carried out his assignments to completion, which was the kind of man the *Company* desperately needed. Yet, Billy knew that for some reason the *Company* had recently turned Jacob Denton Reynolds down. George had said the door could be opened later.

CHAPTER 3

With a vengeance, roiling black clouds dropped their load of wind-driven liquid pellets on the Atlanta interstate rush-hour traffic. Jacob Reynolds braked his dark green Land Rover as an opaque curtain of rain thundered over the vehicle's brightly polished green exterior. Thunder vibrated through the landscape as searing lightning split the cumulonimbus clouds, engulfing a tall pine tree beside the freeway, leaving behind an essence of sulfur. Powerful windshield wipers fought a losing battle against the gushing rivulets streaming over the lightly tinted green windshield.

Jacob leaned forward trying to see the lane lines. Traffic was coming to a halt and he could barely see the taillights of the car ahead. Sweat popped out on his forehead and his first instinct was a primitive panic to escape. He chanced a fast glance in the right rearview mirror and saw a slight space as a car passed on his right. He whipped the Rover over, causing another driver to brake and swerve into the emergency lane. Jacob raced the Rover over onto the emergency lane as the blast of a horn by an eighteen wheeler scattered the cars ahead. Gunning the Rover, Jacob took the grassy sloping hill beside the freeway in four-wheel drive, as the careening truck rammed cars on the freeway exactly where he had been.

As abruptly as it had begun, the fast moving storm moved on and the sun sent a blast of blinding white light, illuminating the deadly scene. A snaking column of flashing red taillights ran down the queue of traffic as far as the eye could see.

"Mother of God!" Jacob said to himself as he sat momentarily stunned at the scene of disaster below him. Then taking a hunting knife from the center console pocket, he jumped from the Rover. Half running, half sliding he quickly made his way down the bank to a smoking car where a young woman was trying desperately to free two children trapped in their car seats in the crushed back seat. Pulling and kicking the door farther open, Jacob slashed the seatbelts and pulled the children to safety. He carried one child while directing the young mother to carry the other to the grassy slope, away from any possible explosion.

That old eerie feeling that had kept him safe through many firefights again made him aware of danger. Not ignoring the danger, but continuing from car to car, he was glad to see many quick thinking drivers had turned off their ignitions and were calming the occupants who were unable to get out. Still the feeling of danger persisted.

Scanning the area, he saw a man glaring at him. The man was small, not more than five-foot-five. There was something familiar about his stance, about the way he held his head, but not his face. Jacob had seen this man before. The man had a cut over his right eyebrow and his left eye was already swollen shut. The sick truth hit Jacob so suddenly it shocked him. He had been the intended victim! His quick move to the emergency lane had thwarted their effort. Unbuttoning the top button of his shirt he whipped off his tie. The man had been walking toward him, but now he hesitated. Jacob did not turn; he just let his peripheral vision keep the man in sight. He had read the body language. The man turned suddenly and walked back to his truck.

Watching him go, Jacob knew he could research the accident report for the man's name. Stooping down, he reassured a man trapped in a car that had folded fore and aft like an accordion, that help was only moments away. Sirens screamed, a helicopter hovered. From one flipped trunk, Jacob grabbed a fire extinguisher and ran toward a blazing fire.

An hour later, exhausted, dirty, clothes disheveled, he climbed back to his vehicle. The four-wheel-drive took the bank going down with ease. Steering around the wrecked cars and debris to the clear road ahead, Jacob shook with rage. Those people were all hurt because some SOB wanted him dead. All that pain inflicted on innocent people. Why hadn't he killed the bastard? His adrenaline was pumping. When he had seen the man coming at him, that old feeling had slipped into gear.

War teaches many lessons, and Jacob had survived three tours in Vietnam. He was confident in his ability, although not cocky. That should be enough to give him some ego, yet he knew that in a second he could be gone just like his friend, who had been sitting right beside him in the Huey. One instant he was there laughing and talking, the next instant he was gone. Jacob shuddered, the mental recall too vivid.

Again caught up in traffic, he adjusted the air conditioning and slipped a tape into the deck. The smooth humorous words by Jim Croce's "Big Bad Leroy Brown" usually made him laugh, but not today.

Taking the next exit, he pulled into the first Quick Stop, filled the gas tank and bought a Gatorade, sucking it down while watching to see if he had been followed.

His mind reviewed the letter of rejection he had received from The Company. Probably it was because of his IRS problems, but even that could be used as cover. What was the matter with them?

Reviewing the disaster of his disbarment in his mind, he wondered if there was anything he could have done differently. It read like a plot for a novel. He had been thoroughly prepared for his day in court in the case of Marlow vs. Brown, but he had missed it altogether. An old classmate had shown up the day before, insisting they go for a drink. Jacob knew he was drinking too much, way too much, but it was something in that last drink that kept him out of circulation for two days. The trial date arrived and passed as he lay in a drugged stupor in a sleazy hotel, while Hill, Marlow and Hardy got a ruling that cost his client over a million dollars. His client then sued him for malpractice and reported him to the Bar for an ethical violation. He had no way to prove that he had been drugged, for even to try would only have shown he had an excess of alcohol in his blood and brought another count against him.

When two fake clients showed up with perfect paperwork, with none of his notations, but a damned near perfect copy of his signature, it was the end. If he could find the artist who copied his signature then he could turn this disbarment business around. He knew nothing was over until he said it was over — he *was* the 'fat lady'.

Half of the million was subsequently awarded to Armond Barfus & Associates, for fees incurred in researching the case. Jacob Reynolds had been had, and he knew it was dirty. He just couldn't figure out the why or the who. If it was Barfus and his cronies, they had no fucking idea the kind of tiger they had by the tail. He walked back to his vehicle, hoping someone actually was following him. It would give him satisfaction for the deep anger filling his gut. A low, primal growl escaped his lips.

He had caught the cowardly friend who had drugged him and the man was recuperating in Grady Hospital. Naturally, he had talked. It had not taken much persuasion. A man named Jerry Wall had given him five thousand; he had been cheap! However, he would not enjoy the money. The word was out and he would be lucky to live through his recuperation. Now Jacob needed to find Jerry Wall.

Traffic had thinned somewhat as Jacob shifted the dark green machine into gear, following the car ahead until he could maneuver and get off at the next street. Fifteen miles later, he turned into his driveway and stopped at the gate. He leaned out and started to open the front of his mailbox, then had second thoughts. Instead, he got out and carefully checked everything. He tied a piece of string to the flap on the mailbox and walked off twenty feet, then pulled the door open. Nothing happened, so after waiting a few more minutes he got his mail. Better safe than sorry.

The driveway cut through a field of clover, then climbed up through dense woods. Dogwoods, showing their majestic deep red leaves of fall, lined the drive, backed by the moss green boughs of evergreens. Raindrops sparkled on all the trees and the cool smell of cedar assailed his senses. He was home. Parking on the pebble drive, he checked the house for any sign of illegal entry. "Just because I'm paranoid," he mumbled.

He walked through the great room, then through the kitchen. Snatching a package from the refrigerator, he went out onto the back deck, which overlooked miles of forest with the Atlanta skyline seemingly tiny in the hazy distance. Lighting the gas grill, he unwrapped the meat, waited for the grill to heat then slapped the steak on the sizzling grid. Closing the lid, he leaned against the railing and glanced through the mail. Ten minutes later, he turned the steak and walked to the refrigerator for a Bud, carrying it back out into the late afternoon cool. Lifting the lid on the grill, he forked the steak, wrapped a napkin around the bone, and then ate the thick T-bone straight. It brought a flashback of killing monkeys in the jungles of Panama.

A huge mastiff bounded up the steps and came to a panting halt beside Reynolds' chair, patiently waiting for the bone. The half shepherd, half mastiff was content and calm, so Jacob knew his acreage was secure. Stark was trained only to eat what he provided or what the dog killed for himself. Had anyone been there while he was gone, Stark would have whined and crawled when he returned.

The black and brown mongrel, as a tailless puppy, had been wandering beside the road when Jacob stopped and opened the door. The puppy had tried frantically to get up and in the Rover. He had picked the puppy up and put it beside him on the seat. They had been together ever since.

He pitched the bone and the dog caught it in midair, then settled down on the deck next to the steps, its powerful jaws crushing and snapping.

Too keyed up about the wreck to relax, knowing it had been an attempt to end his life, he felt edgy. All those bloody, helpless people! It left him with a heavy-headed feeling of frustration and guilt, for what he did not know. The steak and the Bud had not helped. The sky was dark and threatening and it would rain again sometime during the night, but he decided to chance it and go for a workout.

Pulling off his shirt as he walked to the closet in his bedroom, he dropped the shirt on the washer in the hallway. From the small closet he pulled out a pair of well-worn Marine utilities. For the occasion, ex-attorney, retired Lt. Colonel Jacob "D.R." Reynolds turned himself back into Dead Reckon (No ex about that!) and headed for his favorite forest. The only difference was he didn't carry anything in his pack but a shovel and some power bars. He had a knife and a few other little goodies in specially stitched pockets, but this was a peaceful workout. He sought only to better his own abilities and work out his frustration.

Driving down a back road from his house, he continued for two miles, then parked on a dirt road on a low ridge with a large acreage of forest near a little subdivision. He needed the possibility of people to keep his senses sharp, having a need to observe but not be seen, to know he was still able to move about undetected and unsuspected.

Slipping into the foliage, all his troubles took second place as he concentrated on becoming a part of the shadows around him. Following a downward slope to the bottom of the ridge, he noticed a small animal and decided to try to follow without the animal sensing his presence.

Chapter 4

Only an occasional pale orange glow from the tip of his Romeo y Julieta Churchill cigar revealed the tall, slightly stooped man standing back from the street under an old scaly bark tree. He rolled the mild, mellow cigar across his teeth from one side of his mouth to the other in angry annoyance. The woman was late.

A cool breeze rippled the rich green kudzu winding up tree trunks and through branches, then cascading to the ground, a living curtain between the man and the street, effectively shielding him from any curious passersby. Only a strip of light on the horizon was left of the overcast October day. The dark did not bother him. The streetlight would be sufficient for his needs.

The cigar, his ritual extravagance, was at its midpoint and finished, so far as he was concerned. Pushing leaves aside with one toe of his Larado snake skin boots, he dropped the half-cigar and ground it into the damp mulch, then raked the leaves back in place. He grinned, pleased with himself; not even a trace.

He had been paid in advance. With his reputation, no one would dare do otherwise, as he has never failed to carry out a contract. An annoyed flicker pulled his face into a squint. Gordon had been stacking them up for him lately; the bastard knew he didn't like to hurry a job. For the past year he had thought of retiring. He didn't need the money. With a trunk full buried in the garden and another in the attic, he no longer did it for the money. Rubbing his crotch, he reluctantly concluded there was no way he could ever stop doing this.

The ego of self-satisfaction had long since swelled to encompass his entire being. No one had any idea he even existed. He had never moved, never applied for a loan or credit of any kind. He paid his taxes on the farm on time and had improved it to his satisfaction. Unnoticed and left alone, it would be beyond his lifetime before any development reached his rural area. He smiled. *I'm the invisible man. I can do anything; there's nobody with the knowledge, cunning or intelligence to stop me. I am invincible!*

Anticipating the headlines, his mouth pulled in a tight smile. Damn! He really enjoyed those headlines. There was always an astonished uproar at yet another drive-by shooting. The police would pull in every neighborhood kid with a record, and he would be long gone.

Not a handsome man, just a vain one, Ron had never gotten close enough to anyone for them to let him know. Tonight, in the shadows, his lank gray hair had fallen to a point between watery blue eyes that scanned the woods constantly. A new brown wool sweater hung loose across broad shoulders, held up by an aging angular frame that, but for the bulging beer belly, some would call bony.

A sudden thought of the mother he never knew came to mind. Strange for him to think of her, for she had died at his birth—or so his father had said. "The bastard probably killed her." He spoke out loud, without realizing it, he was so engrossed in his thoughts.

He had felt his father's hard hand of abuse throughout his childhood, until that fateful Sunday forty years ago. Knocked to the dirt for some minor infraction, his hand had closed over a fist-sized rock; an anger built up from years of abuse had taken hold. The rock was warm in his hand. He waited for the next blow, grabbed his father's arm and slammed the rock into his temple. Up close he had seen the surprise and disbelief as the man slowly crumpled to the ground.

He had dropped the rock and run to the woods. All night he moved from place to place, hearing noises that he recognized and some he felt to be his dad hunting him with the rifle he kept in the truck. At first light, he angled back to where they had camped, too tired now to care whether his dad killed him or not. From the safety of the woods he was surprised to see the man still on the ground where he had left him. He didn't need the circling buzzards to tell him the man was dead. He lay face down in the dirt and the ants were doing their job. Grabbing a handful of shirt he tried to turn the dead man over, but the body was already stiff.

His stomach churned, sweat ran in rivulets into his eyes, the shock of what he had done overwhelmed him and he gagged again and again. He went to the lake and walked in, intending to drown himself, but the cold water shocked him into reality. *No one need know. I can handle this*, he thought. He walked out of the water and to the truck. He got a shovel and found a gully deep enough, dug it deeper, cleaning it out. He dragged the body by the dark blue coveralls to the freshly dug grave and started to shovel dirt over the body. Then he remembered the wallet.

Scrambling down into the gully, he tried not to think. Bile rose in his throat as he hurriedly removed the thick wallet connected to a chain snapped to a grommet in the side of the front pocket. He had an eerie feeling of triumph as he climbed back out of the makeshift grave. The tormentor was gone—he was free! As he shoveled dirt, threw in stones and brush, he began to plan his future.

Retrieving the fish cage, he drove himself home, cleaned and cooked the fish, cleaned up and went to bed. The next day he caught the school bus as usual.

He had just fed the horses, thinking he would sell them because he was tired of cleaning out the stalls. He had finished breakfast and was drinking a cup of coffee. It was exactly one year since he had killed his father. The man had not even been missed! He sat down and laughed until he cried. At seventeen he had learned his first lesson. Killing could be done without reprisal. That his dad had been a loner with no friends and a bitter old man had made it easy. But continuing his father's work had not been easy. Keeping the farm in shape so that no one would notice, while doing his own schoolwork, had been difficult. But he had managed; after all, the farm was his now.

When the grocer finally asked about the man who had been his customer for over fifteen years, he made up a story. "He got sick, so I took him to my aunt in Alabama. She took him to the doctor, who said it was a stroke. He died two days later. He left me the farm, and I'm taking care of everything." There had been no more questions.

He shook his head. He didn't like remembering, but other thoughts took shape. He graduated from high school and took a job in a bar ten miles away. No drugs or booze for him; it brought unwanted attention. That was where his real career had begun.

It wasn't just a summer storm; the wind was whipping rain crosswise and slamming it into the windows on the southwest side of the restaurant. People were stopping to get out of the storm and the restaurant was full. Only a few truckers were in the bar behind the restaurant, although it would soon be full. He didn't want to work, but the farm taxes had to be paid. While carrying a heavy tray of clean beer mugs to the bar, a trucker tripped him and groped his ass as he fell. Gripped by an insane fury he could not control, but even now vividly recalled, he had grabbed the broken handle of a mug.

It had taken four other truckers to get him off the man. Then they almost killed the guy themselves before the bartender wielding a baseball bat got the man out and sent him by car to the emergency room, his leg near his groin laid open like a slab of fresh meat.

A few days later Gordon pulled a mug of beer and sat down beside Ron. He related how amazed he had been at how well Ron had fought and how calm and cool he had been later as he sat in a booth drinking a cup of coffee. Gordon didn't say how glad he had been to see that the boy showed no remorse, just silent satisfaction. That's when Gordon had decided Ron was just the sort of man he had recently been asked to find. The trucker was an outsider who got what he deserved.

"My Dad taught me how to protect myself." It had been spoken with grim humor and a casualness only experience could convey.

"All of us are witness to that, Ron. You hold your own very well. I know someone who may be able to see you never have to wash a dish again. Are you interested?"

"The answer has to be yes!" He grinned at Gordon, and from then on it was smooth sailing. That had been his first hit and it had been a woman. He had buried her. The next time, he was interrupted by some kids who decided to play in the wrong place. He didn't want to be seen, so he had to leave the body. The write-up in the newspaper was completely speculative and so totally unrealistic that from then on he stayed around for a couple of days, curious to see what the reporters would come up with each time.

Twice there had been no report the next day or the day after and he had left, an uneasy feeling nagging at him. Had he left something behind? He had felt let down, as though he had failed even when he collected the money.

A faint noise arrested his thoughts, instantly grabbing his attention. He was used to small animal noises on the farm. Searching the woods, it didn't take him long to spot the yellow tabby cat scratching among the leaves. He sighed with relief. Bright halogen lights pierced the encroaching darkness sweeping the woods. The cat jumped onto a pile of leaves, then scrambled off to scratch her claws on the nearest tree. Another car rounded the curve and turned into the driveway in front of a house across the street.

Lifting a short stock rifle with scope and silencer to his eye, he sighted on the car and on the walkway leading to the neatly landscaped small white clapboard house. A feeling of power coupled with excitement warmed his stomach. Trained concentration numbed him to everything but the woman in his sights. Nothing could stop him now! Thirty-eight years of experience had taught him that he was the perfect assassin.

A bug fluttered before his eyes, and then used the gunsight for a landing pad. The cat shuffled leaves behind the tree. He lowered the gun to remove the bug. The woman picked up her packages, leaned over to get her purse from the floorboard and reached for the door. The fear was almost tangible; a monks cowl of shivers prickled her head, racing down her spine. She looked around apprehensively.

Ron flicked the bug from the gunsight and began to raise the gun back to his shoulder. A faint odor of leaf mold reached his senses a fraction of a second too late as strong hands snapped his neck in one smooth powerful motion. The gun fell silently from his hand as he slid to the ground, a look of permanent astonishment on his face.

The car door opened and two small, softly booted feet touched the pavement; the woman adjusted her packages and closed the car door with her hip. Bright green eyes followed her progress. He waited until she was inside then turned to look at the body at his feet.

Stooping down, he straightened the body out and put the man's gun aside. He was amazed at what he had done. A warrior's ability to analyze a situation and act had clicked into overdrive. He spoke quietly to himself. "Damn, D.R.! Shouldn't you have given this guy a chance?" He shook his head from side to side. "No way could that woman deserve the fate that man was about deal."

Putting all recriminating thoughts aside, he methodically searched the man's pockets, finding two cigars in a solid gold case with no initials, a set of keys, fingernail clippers and a sharp hunter's folding knife. Then he noticed something unusual. Pulling up the brown sweater, he unbuttoned the man's shirt and found a money belt so stuffed it looked as if the man had a beer belly. He whistled softly. No doubt about it, this was a hit. The dead man was a killer for hire. Now there would be one less monster running loose.

He unfastened the money belt, stuffed it in his pack, took the wallet and keys and dragged the body to a low place between two trees. Taking a folding shovel from his backpack, he buried the man. What he had done needed no remorse, no explanation. More than ever he knew he had done the right thing. Covering the grave with forest mulch, he hoped the night's forthcoming rain would further wipe out any sign of disturbance.

He turned to look back at the house. Tomorrow, he thought, I'll drive by and get the address. Someone wants that little lady very dead. A wry grin tilted his mouth, thinking that the coward who had hired the shooter would get that money right down the back of his neck. That money would pay the expense of one sweet investigation.

He tracked the shooter's path back to where he had parked his truck. It was a brand new dark green Dodge Ram. D.R. whistled under his breath. It was a beauty, with deeply tinted windows. He carefully observed the truck for some time to be sure there was no accomplice. He knew most assassins worked alone but that was not always true. Cowards sometimes needed backup.

After a while, he unlocked the truck and stepped back. Then he carefully searched the cab and behind the front seat in a special custom made pocket closed with Velcro, so neatly made he had missed it the first time, he found the shooter's briefcase.

The seat on the passenger side opened quietly to his gentle probing touch. Inside was an arsenal of weapons, including grenades. The killer had been a one-man army. Police monitoring radios, radar detector, a camera to fit on a rifle sight, too much to leave for neighborhood kids to find. Besides, he might find a use for this stuff.

After carefully examining the engine with his night vision goggles and sliding under the truck to examine the undercarriage for explosives, he decided the truck was clean. Only then did he drive it back to the road about a mile from his Rover. He would put it in his garage for possible future use.

Something powerful had propelled him out this evening. He had serious career problems to address, but a nagging restlessness had spurred him to work out. It was his way of keeping his mind sharp and his body keen. He had seen the tabby and tried to be as quiet as the cat. He almost was. Is there a God after all, he wondered?

In the dark of the moonless night, the camouflaged man slowly and carefully made his way back to his dark green Land Rover. He removed his camouflage outfit and drove part of the way home, then hiked back and brought the truck, locking it in the garage. Then he hiked back to the Rover and drove to the nearest car wash and thoroughly cleaned the vehicle. Later at home, after he had washed off the physical dirt, he spread newspaper on the kitchen table, put on surgical latex gloves and went through the briefcase.

He was stunned by what he found. There was a record of every hit the man had made for thirty-eight years. Some of the names he recognized. The police should have this, he thought. But how can I do this? As an attorney, he knew it would imply malice murder. It would not matter what the hired killer had done; it would only matter that he had killed a man—a man with no conscience. So, he had pulled the lever in the gas chamber, administered the needle, what did it matter? The man would have gone on killing for money the rest of his life.

There were three children in the book. The horror of the cold-blooded killer nauseated him. To D.R., killing was only necessary if it helped to save lives, not to take them.

That man had been the first since Vietnam, but he had to admit, he might not be the last. Had he taken time to analyze the situation, maybe he would not have done it in that way, realizing his frustration level was out of sight. Maybe he should have made the man talk. But time had been of the essence; the game had already been in motion.

His own mortality of soul bothered him. His conscience had been a nagging presence, at least until he had read the shooter's notebook. War was where you found it; he knew that through him justice had triumphed.

One name at the front of the book was Gordon Land. Evidently Gordon was his contact. The killer's ego outsmarted Gordon. It was evident from the killer's diary that the man wanted notoriety should he be caught, and he wanted to take Gordon down with him. Was it his revenge for having sold himself to the dark side?

D.R. started to burn the book because if he were caught with it in his possession, he would be thought to be the killer. But if he burned it, those people who hired the man to kill for them would go free. That man had been a creature that Hollywood in all its imagination could not produce. It certainly had not been human.

Who could he give the book to who would take it seriously and do something about it? Aha! Annabelle Livingston, his own special federal investigator. He smiled. She'll really sink her teeth into this one. The book wasn't much evidence, but could be enough to get a confession.

He wondered if the shooter had a family, and where he had lived. It would be logical that he had more weapons at home. Perhaps later he would explore that possibility. Maybe in the truck pocket he would find a driver's license.

He pulled on a cap and headed again for his Rover. He drove to Annabelle's house, taking a paved lane from a back road to within walking distance. He had installed the alarm system, so he knew how to disconnect it. He let himself in so quietly she could have been standing in the hallway and she would not have heard him.

He propped the briefcase open on her desk, along with the book and gun, then left as quietly as he had entered, pleased that he had missed the squeaky board in the library. He left a rough disconnect on the alarm system that the police would find and that Annabelle would know was beneath his expertise. Driving home he decided his first priority would be to learn the name of the assassin's target and begin an investigation into who wanted her dead.

Back home he turned on the alarms, went upstairs and turned down his bed. Then he put a rolled pillow under the covers and turned off the light. Taking his poncho liner, he went downstairs and rolled up in the poncho behind the sofa. He hoped there would be no nightmares tonight.

Chapter 5

Buffeted by the wind, the girl's short brown hair sparked copper highlights when touched by the streetlights. She ran out of the woods and across the parking lot toward him. To his left, three men with rifles were lifting and aiming . . . only instead of the splat of bullets, the distant shrill ringing of a telephone brought Jacob's eyes snapping open.

Muscles ached where he had forgotten he had muscles. He eased his five-foot-eleven body from behind the sofa. Like every other caffeine addict, he badly needed a cup of coffee.

By habit, he checked the second alarm system, the one that told him if the first had been tampered with. Nobody had to tell him he was paranoid. Besides, only one person would be calling him this early. He picked up the phone on the tenth ring.

"Hello."

"Jacob Reynolds! Did you leave that mess on my desk last night?"

"Who the hell is this?"

"You know damned well who it is!"

"Annabelle? What time is it?" He looked at the wall clock that read six-fifteen. "When did you start getting up so early?"

"Time doesn't matter. I woke with a start about five a.m. and went down for a hot toddy, you know the kind I like with a shot of bourbon? Well, I noticed the door to my library was open and guess what I found on my desk?"

"Annabelle, cut to the chase. I haven't the faintest

idea what you're talking about. If I had come over there I would have rung the bell, just like always."

"Don't get smart with me, Jacob. Nobody but you could come and go from my house without making noises. What do you expect me to do with this stuff?"

"What stuff are you talking about? Damn it, Annabelle, I haven't even had a cup of coffee, let alone know what is going on at your house."

"Get that super ass of yours over here right now. I have something to show you, and I'm making coffee."

With that she clicked off, leaving Jacob grinning and shaking his head. "Well, I guess I'd better get my *super ass* over there before she sends the troops after me. She does make good coffee—among other things."

He turned the shower on hot. It always took the water a while to get there from the water heater in the basement. He could do without the shock of cold water this morning. Last night had been extremely rough on his physique as well as his mind.

Had he the conceit to analyze his reflection in the mirrored wall, he would have seen a face any mother would love: dimples, bright green eyes, deep lines chiseled around a wide handsome mouth always quick to humor. In all, a handsome man of fifty-two, hair still intact and thick, but he wasn't thinking of any of this. His ego had been honed and mellowed by adversity and experience long years past.

Someone watching—a woman perhaps—would have been impressed by the still muscular body with a taut stomach leading to a relaxed component that fell like a waterfall from a curly brown mat.

He stayed in the shower longer than usual, letting the hot water release the tension in his neck and shoulders. It would not be an easy morning, but it could be fun. He grinned at the thought of Annabelle puzzling over the cache. She would know that he would never be as sloppy as whoever cut her alarm system. She may think she knows I did it, he thought, but she will never really be sure.

Forty-five minutes later he turned into Annabelle's

old brick driveway under the shady canopy of the big oak trees and parked under the portico right in front of the door. This was not a sneak-in call. Annabelle opened the door before he rang the bell. She was dressed in jeans and a sweatshirt with "Kick Ass With Class" in gold letters across the front, surrounded by beautiful multicolored orchids.

At forty-three she was a looker: tight hips, thin waist and ample bosom, tall but not too tall, and aggressive in business and pleasure. She had instigated their two-year love affair and she had ended it with an "Until later time clause," since she was thinking about running for public office. When she had made that statement, he had said, "When elephants fly," knowing there was no way she would honor that decision.

Some men needed to brag about their conquests, but not Jacob. Anything a lady chose to bestow, he chose to cherish quietly. Content in his manhood, he had no need to prove himself at the corner bar. That kind of braggadocio was for the boys.

"How dare you scare the shit out of me like that!"

"Damn! You're beautiful with your eyes flashing fire like that."

"Jacob! This isn't a social call. This is serious. If you didn't leave that mess then who did?"

"First, I need to know what *that mess* is, then some breakfast would be appreciated. There's a huge crater where my stomach should be. You do still make the best breakfast in the world, don't you?"

"It's ready. I cooked while I waited for you, but first look at that stuff on my desk and give me your opinion. Are you still saying you didn't come in here last night?"

"I believe the lady is getting the picture."

Annabelle shook her head, probably not believing a word he said.

"Give me a cup of coffee and I'll tell you any truth you want to hear, as I see it. Then I will look at anything you want me to. Damn those are beautiful orchids."

"Your opinion is all I need this morning. I don't have time to do your manhood justice." Her voice had softened and the iris of her eyes dilated. "Dammit, Jacob! Look what you're doing to me. Now you'll have to come back tonight, maybe around eleven. Even so, I will be hotter than a tiger all day in anticipation. But first I have to have dinner with the district attorney and his wife tonight."

She turned abruptly and walked into the library. He smiled and nodded, then followed the gentle swaying of her narrow hips, his own imagination looking forward to the evening pleasures.

On the desk were the open briefcase, book and gun just as he had left them.

"Is it wired?"

"Explosives? No! I didn't even think of that! It's all so open, I haven't touched anything. It was just like that when I walked in at five this morning."

Jacob picked up a letter opener and opened the book. He read the first few names. "What is this, Annabelle? Two of those people were killed. I remember reading about it in the paper. One was a judge, the other a policeman." He continued to turn pages. "Here's another! That man was CEO of a company that went bankrupt. It was in the paper maybe two years ago. Somebody keeping a record of murders . . . Shit! Is this what I think it is?"

"Just what do you think it is, Jacob?"

"Judging from the gun with the silencer and short stock, I would say this book contains the records of an assassin's hits from 1960. I'd have to check with the police, but it seems to be the case. It just appeared here as though by magic, huh?"

"As though you didn't know."

"Annabelle." His voice was firm, the look in his eyes hard in its intention. "I don't know anything about this."

"Okay! That's what you say, Jacob. But there's not another person alive who could have put that there. This is all just too easy. It worries me that it may be a trap. Where is the assassin? He sure as hell didn't leave this here."

"My opinion, for what it's worth," he began, looking directly into her worried eyes, noticing the lids were slightly swollen, "is that the assassin will never be found." He placed his hands on her shoulders to emphasize his words. "This would not be here if he were still alive, you can bet your steely on it. Whoever left this probably saved a lot of lives. Just be grateful, Annabelle. Some concerned citizen did you a favor. Did you look at the last entry?"

She went to the desk, picked up the letter opener he had put down and turned the pages. "Norman Lee, the DA in Memphis! My God! I'll have to call and warn him. Can you believe that man operated all these years and no one caught up with him?"

"I'm willing to bet the man never even got a traffic ticket. Now, do I get that promised coffee and breakfast? Have I satisfied your curiosity?"

"Yes, now that I know you killed him, I'm at peace, thankful that there is some justice in the world. I know you deny any connection and I won't make any. Come on, I'll make you your favorite omelet."

Jacob carried his plate and coffee out to the atrium and set them down on the glass-topped table. He pulled up a blue wicker chair and sat down. Huge yellow roses bloomed in profusion in the center of the atrium.

"Dear God! Annabelle, I had forgotten about your roses. They're more beautiful than I remembered. I'll have to start coming over earlier; it's hard to see them when I come in the dark and leave in the dark."

"When we both retire, then we'll have time to enjoy them. Meanwhile, eat your breakfast."

"You won't even let a man be poetic. I was about to quip that even in all their beauty they can't hold a candle to you. Does that get me a second cup of coffee?"

"Almost, but you can keep trying."

"You've done it again, that omelet was almost perfect."

"Oh! Not perfect huh? Well next time make your own."

Annabelle watched the beginning of his slow mischievous grin. She knew that expression well and waited for the punch line.

"If you were perfect you'd be a saint and I couldn't make love to you." He walked around the table and slid his hands over the orchids.

"Jacob, take your coffee and bring the cup back tonight. The maid will be here in ten minutes and you're not a ten-minute man."

"You got that right! Orchids and roses deserve time to enjoy."

She put a hand behind his head and pulled him down for a kiss. "See you tonight?"

He nodded. "Eleven o'clock sharp."

The warm fuzzy look in her eyes slowly disappeared and the eyes of a huntress emerged. She reached for the phone, a hunter on the prowl.

"Better have it all dusted for fingerprints," he called over his shoulder while walking back to the kitchen. He poured more coffee in one of Annabelle's mugs with lettering on the side that read: "My way is the only way."

It was time to find out the name of the woman in the little white house, the one the shooter was after. She was awfully close to home.

Chapter 6

The file didn't weigh enough to offset the five years of constant work to acquire his degree, Jacob thought as he placed the folder on the edge of his old maple rolltop desk. He would not store these papers just yet. Soon, very soon, he would find a way to reverse that disbarment decision, even if he had to choke it out of Barfus.

He had always gone the extra mile, volunteering to take extra survival school training, jump school, naval air and gunfire controller programs, jungle school and the one that would later cause him much grief, Forward Air Controller, commonly known as FAC school. No right thinking, self-respecting Marine Aviator would volunteer for that *grunt stuff*. His explanation was simple: he thought being a Marine officer meant supporting and protecting those ground Marines in any way conceivable. However, there was some elitism in Marine Aviation and maybe he thought there should be. But since his ego was even bigger than the ego of most fighter pilots, he made himself singular by that additional effort. He sure as hell marched to a different drummer, as his parents were so often told.

At the moment, he had a leash on his anger, but with everything that was happening, he didn't know how long that would last. He tried to concentrate on the work at hand while waiting for Inez to check the voting records at the courthouse for the name of the assassin's target at number 19 Finn Street, and the name of the shooter and his address from the auto tag. He couldn't do anything until he had that information.

He walked the floor, thinking. What he was about to do was just another form of warfare. Could he fight his own war in good conscience? Killing the shooter had been instinctive. What he now wanted to do would be premeditated. He had once done it for the American people, useless as it had been. Could he not now do it for himself and for this innocent woman? But how did he know she was innocent? She had to be, otherwise nobody would put out that much attention or money to destroy her.

Why didn't they do it the usual way: simply destroy her credibility by planting false information on her record? That was easy enough to do. Fifty dollars would buy a little insertion of false information from a clerk on drugs — a hell of a lot less expensive than the shooter. Or they could have drugged her, taken forced, compromising photographs and then sold them — even made money on the deal. They could have reported to the FBI that she had, in private conversation or in counseling, threatened the President. That way, she would be lucky to ever get a job again. Why was is it so important that she be killed? Did people of importance know her? Was her intelligence so respected that they were afraid she would expose something they didn't want anyone to know? Bingo!

His mind flashed back to before he had set foot on Quantico for the first time, before he had been subtly coerced through Kennedy's moving speeches. What would his life have been like had he not become a Marine, not gone to war? No doubt he would not have become a *pain-in-the-ass* idealist as he claimed to be. Nor would he have experienced the flash, the excitement, the horror or the depression of war. He couldn't imagine what he would have been. In his teens his greatest desire had been to fly, so maybe he would have been a commercial pilot. One thing for sure, he would never have killed anyone, a delusion perhaps, but he could see no other possibility, given the life he would have led.

What kind of argument was that for compulsory service? Was it socially, spiritually, economically or psychologically reasonable that some people should be forced to do what others wanted to do? Did I want to do what I forced myself to do? No! Other than the men and women who died in the line of fire doing their jobs, did some prefer to die in war rather than kill another person?

Continuing his metaphysical assessment, Jacob wondered: Do people realize they are creating warrior-killers when they send young men into battle? In the war game when leaders move pieces on their chessboard, deliberately making some pawns and some knights, how do they decide which will be which? It was true that war created heroes, if only from the necessity to survive, or to help their fellow Marines survive, or for a real devotion to protecting country and family. He knew from experience that if a peaceful man was put into a ring with a vicious killer, if he survived the first assault, he would fight back.

These men we put in death's way, make into heroes, are they simply our alter egos, what all people need, because they cannot bear to be their own protectors? Is that why people flee their own country rather than fight for their own homes, because they can't stand to kill? Do Mr. or Mrs. America ever think about what they expect of others?

Strange that warriors are the public's heroes. Why not teachers and statesmen? Probably because the warrior will do what the average citizen's ethical good religious conduct or cowardice — take your pick — doesn't allow him to do, fearing that if he kills, he will go to hell. So it eases his conscience to send others to do his killing for him, hoping in the game to keep clean from killing, to assure a place in heaven, yet enjoying the safety and prosperity that the *Monster Heroes* have kept safe for him, then condemning them for that very act. What a mess! The pariah syndrome; police get it all the time.

He was one of those creatures — trained, used and released. Yet, somehow, he felt that the God who created us was far more intelligent than the 'holier than thou's' gave Him credit for. Or was he just rationalizing, hoping to protect his own soul or at least his sanity?

The ringing of the telephone jolted him from his philosophical thoughts. It was Inez with the name of the assassin's target. Jacob was surprised to learn that she worked for a legal firm, Donnelley & Associates, across the street from his new enemy, Armond Barfus and Ass. He preferred the abbreviated *Ass* in reference to Barfus because it suited the man so much better.

"Inez, you're an angel. If you weren't such a good friend, I'd ask you to lunch."

"Joe and I are very upset about what happened to you, Jacob. Remember, we're here for you any time you need us. I'd rather deliver that other information you need."

"Thanks for the consideration, Inez, I'll wait for you."

"I'll be there sometime before five. See you then."

So, Big Joe knew about his problem and they were there for him. His eyes deceived him as a tear formed. Damn! He could take anything, except kindness; that, he was not used to. It was just like Joe to stand by him in his trouble. He experienced a brief flashback of Joe running, zigzagging, carrying an injured Marine, bullets whining in the air. Joe had made it to the chopper and handed the wounded Marine up to the waiting corpsman just as a bullet struck him below the elbow. The crew chief dragged him into the chopper by his right arm, putting a tourniquet on his left arm as they thundered out of there. He never once heard Joe complain. The man Joe rescued had lived, but lost a leg; Joe had lost his arm.

The phone rang again.

"Hello! D.R.! How you doing, asshole? Got your message, what do you need, my man?"

"Irish! I do hope *asshole* is a term of endearment. I sure as hell need some help. Do you have a huge closed truck and someone to pack? I've got a lot of moving to do and I'm not mentally up to doing it myself. Can you send someone over?"

His peripheral vision caught a movement near the door. A tall young man had walked in, his broad shoulders filling the doorway. Seeing that Jacob was on the phone, he leaned against the door facing, waiting for him to finish talking. Maurice crammed his hands into the pockets of his bluejeans, pinning back his old tan corduroy blazer, and waited.

Obviously a young barrister, Jacob thought as he nodded in the young man's direction. He continued his conversation until he was sure Johnny had the proper directions, then gave the young man his full attention.

"Is there something I can do for you?"

"Counselor Reynolds?"

"Ex-Counselor Reynolds, at your service."

"I'm Maurice Thompson." Jacob's face changed subtly from acceptance to disgust, so Thompson quickly continued, "I quit Armond Barfus. I don't know why I'm here except to say that I'm sorry for what happened. That's one reason I quit."

"The colonel had you on a year's trial?"

"Yes. It was up last week. I turned in my letter at the meeting this morning and left."

"Do you know a Mary Leland who works for Donnelley and Associates across the street from the colonel?"

"Yes! She was in research, but they fired her this morning. I saw her leaving. She was crying and I asked her what was wrong. She said Bubba Wall just came in and fired her. He gave her two weeks' severance and told her to leave. Why are you asking?"

"She called just before you showed up, asking for a job. I intend to keep an office, but I won't be practicing law. Do you know what she was working on at Donnelley? I may be able to use her."

"Not being with that firm, I don't know anything about what she worked on, but we talked at the Courthouse Grill a few times. She just researched case information as far as I know. The times we talked, it seemed she was very careful with her data and knew a lot about the law. She has a very good sense of humor, but all told, I really don't know her well. I've heard her name mentioned when we all gather at parties and such, and her opinions elicit a lot of interest. She's very intelligent."

He walked a little farther into the room before continuing, "I didn't have anything to do with your trial, but I heard about it and didn't like what they did. Just being associated with them made me feel guilty. I want you to know that if there is anything I can do to help you get reinstated just let me know."

He held out his hand and Jacob grasped it in his own. "I wish you luck. Where did you say you were going?"

"I didn't, but it's Thomaston. That's my hometown. Old Dean Armani wanted me last year and called me again a month ago. He has his priorities in the right place. We'll make a good team."

"Yes, he sure does!" Jacob laughed. "I've worked with Dean a couple of times. Other lawyers can pull all the fancy stuff they want, but Dean has all the law rules on a silver strand in his head and he quotes them right out of the book. He's a real tiger, a man with integrity. Unusual in a business with little if any of that most desired trait."

"That's true for sure, and one thing I like about him. It will be quite a change from working with the Barfus firm. At least now I know what kind of lawyer I don't want to be. You might want to get in touch with Marge LeVan, Jacob." With that parting note, Maurice grinned, gave Jacob a salute and walked out.

Marge LeVan, huh? Yeah, not a bad idea. Thanks, Colonel, that one sure fell neatly in my lap, Jacob thought as he picked up the old black phone and dialed Mary's number. He waited through four rings and was about to hang up when she answered.

"Is this Mary Leland?"

"Yes?"

"Mary, this is Jacob Reynolds. Maurice Thompson just left my office. He said you left Donnelley this morning. I wonder if you would like to help me do some packing. I'll need everything labeled and it will take someone with knowledge of the law. "

After a few seconds of silence, she answered, "Maurice told you to call me? He's a nice guy. I heard what the colonel did to you. Yes, I'll help you out. If you're packing up your office, it could be a big job."

"That's right, you understand the situation and that's what I need. I will be setting up another office and will also need help at that location. Eighteen dollars an hour cash for the next two weeks; then if you decide to stay on, we'll negotiate. The address is 1722 North Main Street. Can you be here in thirty minutes?"

"Sure! Why not?"

He pulled a roll of Tums from his pocket and popped one in his mouth. His stomach was in a knot and his anger hard to control. What would happen if he snapped? Wasn't he entitled to be upset about what had happened to him this past year? Didn't he have a right to scream and beat his fist against the wall? Maybe, but he knew that if he snapped people would die and he had a list. He was having too much time to think; he needed to keep busy. Not yet sure of his direction, his mind rambled, questioning every aspect of his learned information. Will I be made stronger or weaker when the respected system is questioned with candor or tested by dissent? There was a hell of a lot of dissent racing around his mind right now. Would cost effectiveness and combat proficiency be his exclusive goals? Hell, no! Revenge was his only objective. He wanted to lash out at the enemy but the enemy was elusive. He knew Barfus could be mean, but the piss-ant show-off didn't have the built-in rage to come after him alone. His reasoning mind told him that was an unknown factor, something he was missing. But he would soon solve the equation. He was so angry that he balled his fist so tightly his fingernails cut into his hand.

"Damn!" He looked surprised at the blood oozing from his palm and walked into the bathroom for the first aid kit. He had to cool down, to think rationally, and start on a program. Temper could kill and he didn't want it to be him. He wanted to pull this off without being caught. The questions were: What do I do? How do I do it? Obviously, he could not resort to combat tactics and blow the bastards up, so he must use more subtle, intelligent ways to eliminate those roaches preying on honest men and women. First the people after Mary, then he would go on his own quest.

Jacob knew now it wasn't only his revenge, but the horror at what money had been buying for thirty-eight years. And someone connected with Mary had paid the hitter, someone who was a so-called pillar of the community. He had given Inez the shooter's license plate number and as soon as Inez brought the shooter's name and address, he hoped to find more information leading to the person who had hired the shooter. He would have to get there before Annabelle's troops.

He had the combat skill and experience to start his own private war, but that wouldn't be smart and it could get him locked up fast. He would do it in a more subtle, acceptable way. After all, they did strike the first blow and nobody could ever say that D.R. turned the other cheek. Okay! So now I'm a detective. How do I get the needed information? Just walk up to Mary and say, "Mary, I recently killed an assassin that someone hired to kill you. Do you by any chance know who may have hired him?"

Could it have been Bubba? Why did he fire her? Bubba might use the law badly, but murder a woman . . . surely he wouldn't stoop that low. There had to be a domestic situation here. Correction: Too much money changed hands for it to be domestic, more money than the Queen of Sheba's insurance policy. Too high class a kill, but not a high-class killer.

"Yo! D.R.!" The man pronounced D.R. as "Dar," as did all his buddies.

Jacob turned to see Johnny 'Irish' Michaels walk in with a grin from scar to scar. It was a little lopsided but perfect on his lean, angular face. Short curly orange-gray hair covered his large head and the freckles over his nose insinuated good times were here! "Johnny Michaels—Irish to the core—you old son of a scalded-ass rabid dog!"

They hugged, then stepped back and took a couple of mock punches at one another. "Okay! You need muscle, here it is! He held up one arm, flexing a large bicep. If you hadn't gotten me out of prison, I'd be on the cover of Muscle Man Magazine by now."

"Just think, the first time I saw you, you were a tall skinny drink of water. What ever happened to that West Virginia girl?"

"After Nam, I had changed too much. She no longer suited me. Ah! Might as well tell the truth, she had her eye on the bank, not me. Can't blame her, she wanted everything she never had. That's just the way it goes sometimes. That was a long time ago, Bro—lot of water under the bridge since Nam. What's going on, D.R.?"

"I've been disbarred on a technicality, can't practice law anymore—you probably read it in the paper. So, I gotta move out—find a place of my own. I have one in mind and will see about it this afternoon." He noted Irish had not made any move and still seemed interested.

"A beautiful young lady will be here shortly; her name is Mary Leland. She'll know how to pack everything and label it; she can tell you what to pack with what. That is, if you want to stay. If you do, I'd appreciate your getting her whatever she needs—that is, if you can help me out right now. If you can't, maybe you can recommend someone."

"Got nothing on the agenda just now, and that mention of a pretty lady sounds good. Lead on, buddy."

"I'm negotiating for the old warehouse building on Twenty-first Street. Hopefully we'll close on it Wednesday. It backs up to some woods that will suit my nocturnal ways." He gave Johnny a high five.

"You're going to do something, aren't you D.R.? I've seen you do more for less. What turkey was stupid enough to come after you?"

"Irish, it was one Colonel Armond Barfus of Barfus and Associates. He did a very good job. I'm out of the legal profession."

"Damn! D.R., you jawed us raw about becoming a lawyer. That kept you going. Now this colonel . . . is he really a colonel?"

"Yep! Full bird and arrogant."

"Oh! Holy Mother! One of those, huh? Did he ever walk the jungle?"

"I don't know yet. Just getting on the job. How's the moving business? Does it keep you busy all the time?"

"I've got some good help. All you have to do is call."

"I just did."

A light tap on the door interrupted them. "Hello, I'm Mary Leland. I hope you don't mind." She indicated her jeans and red Georgia Bulldog sweatshirt. "You did say you were moving?"

"You're fine." To himself, Jacob admitted that she was more than fine, she was a pretty lady. He was momentarily speechless, but Johnny had totally lost his smooth calm. His mouth had dropped open like a teenage kid trying to figure out how to ask a girl to the prom. Jacob took in her close-cropped mahogany hair with gray at the temples. Tiny laugh lines edged brown serious eyes with long lashes that gave her a sultry brooding look that quickly crinkled into a smile, bringing sunshine into the room.

He walked toward her, holding out his hand. A flash of her with her head blown away had he not been there skirted through his mind. That would have been a terrible waste. "I'm Jacob Reynolds, and this hunk of brain and muscle is Johnny Michaels. Johnny, meet Mary Leland."

Somehow Johnny was able to come out of his stupor long enough to take her hand and speak a mumbling "Hello," his face slightly red. He smiled as Jacob had never seen him smile and it was returned in kind by Mary, who finally looked at him quizzically until he laughed. With a look that said, "Do I have to" in his eyes, he reluctantly released her hand.

"Mary, Johnny will be your right-hand man. Whatever you need, he will get it for you. Whatever you need lifted, he can handle it. I have to leave to see about an office, so you two can get started. I may not be here when you're ready to leave, Mary, so here's a key, and one for you, Johnny. Irish, walk me out and give Mary a chance to get her bearings."

Halfway to Jacob's car, Johnny's impatience got the best of him. "Okay, D.R.! What's going on?"

"Let's just say a guy who was trying to kill Mary is taking a long overdue dirt nap. No questions on that one. Suffice it to say, she doesn't know. Use that Irish charm; see if you can get her to talk. I want to know who wants to kill her and why."

"My God, D.R.! Who'd wanna kill that beautiful woman?"

"That's what we have to find out. Do you want in?"

"Hell, yes! I'll kill the motherfucker myself!"

"If you're positive about that, keep a lookout, the shooter may have a replacement." Then he grinned. "Try to keep wily wolf in check. She's quite a handsome, intelligent and nice lady."

"Damn! You know me too well." He grinned. "There's something about her, D.R. I'd go the distance for her. Never felt this way before."

"Wanna go on a little recon job with me tonight?"

"Something to do with who's trying to kill Mary?"

"I'm following up on the shooter. Need to check out his place of residence. It could be a little hairy. I'm taking Boom along."

"You can count on me. What time?"

"Call me around five-thirty, I'll know by then where it is and how long it will take to get there. If it's close enough, we go tonight from Boom's."

Irish watched his friend drive away, automatically scanning the area. He rubbed his hands together, then went to his truck and retrieved his .45 automatic. He tucked it under the back waistband of his jeans, clipping it over the waistband and under his jacket.

"Ah! Good times are here again," Johnny mumbled.

Chapter 7

Branches from pecan trees overlapped the narrow rural road, and the overgrown fencerows made signs hard to see and virtually impossible to read, especially in the dark. Boom turned the dark green Dodge Ram right at the old dilapidated country store, its sides plastered with cola and tobacco signs, its two old gas pumps now antique derelicts standing in the middle of a dirt parking lot.

For two miles, D.R., Boom and Irish passed lighted, well-kept farms. A quarter of a mile farther, they slowed to a stop before a narrow dirt track leading between two fence posts. Irish slid silently from the truck and disappeared into the shadows. Returning a few minutes later he motioned them to turn in. A mailbox was stuck back in the thicket to the left of the driveway, faint numbers on its side. The dirt road led through thick scrub oaks that had recently been cut back to widen the entrance.

"Didn't want to scratch his new truck? This has to be the place. Shall we drive on in?"

"Don't think so, D.R. I'll go point and Boom can follow. You wait to bring the truck," Irish said.

They didn't find any booby traps until about a hundred yards farther, where a gate blocked the chert driveway. A strand of nylon filament led to a bunch of cans — a simple alarm, but to what purpose? Dogs? Tying off the nylon they again checked the gate and found nothing, yet Boom waited. Those simple wooden posts were new. No leaders could be seen, which was insignificant, as an alarm could be battery operated or wired underground. He had a feeling that had never before failed him. If there was an alarm, there had to be a way to turn it off from the truck.

In a hole on a post he found a hidden sensor. He went back and had D.R. flick the lights up, then down and up again—nothing happened. "Hit the lights again, D.R., only this time do bright-low-bright-low," Irish said. D.R. did so and after an audible click the gate opened quietly on well-oiled hinges. Then a beam came on, seen only with night goggles, near the bottom shining between the posts across the entrance. "Got another one—now lower the beams." The alarm went off. "That got it, I don't see anything else."

Carefully searching for any other alarm, Johnny and Boom followed the driveway, which was paved starting ten yards inside the gate. They were within sight of the house when the geese attacked, squawking and racing out toward them with necks outstretched. Boom and Irish jumped in the truck. "Man! Those are big geese and I know they can cause a bruise. I got pecked by one as a kid. The cans were to alarm the geese, a simple but effective alarm."

D.R. couldn't keep from laughing. "Man, you two are real warriors, routed by a gaggle of geese."

"Okay, D.R., you take point and I'll drive."

The geese waddled beside the truck, honking loudly. "That blows our quiet entry," Irish said. With a little bottle he sprayed the geese and the honking ceased.

Ahead they saw a house with a barn and a couple of outbuildings. They drove by two cars parked in a dirt-floored shed. There were no fresh tracks leading out of the shed. "It rained the night I found the shooter," D.R. said, "and those cars haven't been moved since before that time."

"House looks pretty quiet; only a night light burning. What do you see with the heat sensors, Boom?" Irish asked.

They waited while Boom scanned the area. "A dog's on the porch. Don't see anyone in the house—no animals in the barn. There's another sensor on the gate beside the back door. See what happens when you flick the lights."

D.R. flashed the bright on and off, then on and the

sensors went off. "That got the gate. Park where the tire marks are — that's probably where he usually parked — then wait a minute. Irish, scan the ground near the back door."

"There's a difference in glow to the left of the top step — something electric there," Irish said. "Here's the sleeping spray for the dog if we need it. Let's go in." The old hound just thumped its tail on the wooden porch floor, without lifting its head. "You hear that? So can anyone inside. Simple alarm, but smart. Most people won't bother a friendly dog. We won't either since nobody's home."

"D.R., look at that! Three locks on that door. Damn! I'll bet he has a sequence. That's probably what I see beside the top step." Boom stooped down to inspect the box on the edge of the porch. It looked like a piece of an old post.

"Ah-ha! It's a roughly made bomb, but it would be very effective. Wires go under the porch. It's not strong enough to blow the house, but strong enough to cause anyone unaware a lot of pain, rigged with roofing nails and shot banked to go out, covering the landing where anybody would have to stand to pick the locks. That would really smart if it hit you, maybe take off a foot. Not professional, very rough, but very effective. Okay! It's off and I don't see any more. Let's go in."

D.R. unlocked the door with the shooter's keys, and they stepped inside. The old house was clean and neat with a musty bacon smell. They checked out the first floor; D.R. found only paid receipts from the past sixty years. He found no records of the man's profession, guessing he took it with him. Irish took the attic. A few minutes later he whistled. D.R. and Boom hurried up the steps. Irish had found a big old trunk hidden under a tarp. "Hey number one, let's check this out. See anything I don't see?"

Boom circled the trunk, then put a tiny charge in the lock. "If there's anything inside we'll know in a minute."

They heard a small *whump.* Boom said, "Well, what have we here? Hey, you guys know anybody needs a loan? Don't think your shooter trusted banks. Must be millions here! Should we take it or leave it for the Feds?"

"Is that a real question?"

"Hell, no!" Irish said, pulling a large thin nylon bag from a pocket. "Fill it up, boys. I'll see if I can find some more bags. Let's get this in the truck. May need it before we're through."

D.R. nudged Irish. "You check for any hidden cameras. I know damned well that he will have one. He may have been simple, but he was thorough."

They had just put the sacks of money in the van when Irish came out carrying three small cameras and two miniature voice-activated tape players. "Guess we'd better do one last sweep and remove any footprints; don't want to leave evidence for the Feds."

"There's a basement, but don't go down there. He was a very sick turkey. I just glanced in and left it as is. Let the Feds have that one. We've seen enough in the past."

Two hours later they sat in Boom's kitchen eating steak and eggs, the money in bags on the floor. They wouldn't bother to count it, just repackage and put it in safety deposit boxes. "Boom, you can be the banker," D.R. said. "We'll take all we need for now. We'll each take a safe deposit box and put in all it will hold. We'll probably have to get one in every bank in the state. Who knows when any one of us will need a good attorney or to pay for a church wedding for one red-faced Irishman?"

"Are you kidding? Irish's getting married?"

"Hell, man! I haven't even asked her yet. You guys don't go and mess it up. Give me a break," Irish said.

"Don't worry, Johnny, we won't interfere, scout's honor. How about another hunk of that sirloin, Boom, and another cup of coffee. Damn! This running around in black underwear works up an appetite."

"Yeah! You know for three still strong over-the-hill commandos, we've done pretty well tonight," D.R. said, as all three raised their coffee cups.

"Between the dark and light the law gives forth a light for those who cannot see . . . for men like you and me," Irish quoted.

In unison, they said "Amen!"

Chapter 8

Harvey Morrow eased out of the Chrysler Imperial and leaned against it to straighten his huge frame and get his breath. He suffered from too much success and excess. Jacob waited for Harvey to walk to him, figuring Harvey needed the exercise.

"Well, Reynolds, have we got a deal?"

"Take off twenty-five thousand and we can sign the papers today. And I will pay you cash."

"Ah! Did I hear right, you said cash?"

"Harvey, you know it's been empty for three years and the town is growing the other way. You can't get top dollar anymore way out here. It'll take a ton of money to fix it up."

"You have it, Jacob, I've wanted to do something for you for a long time. I knew you wouldn't take money and I've already said *thank you*, but now I can do something. You've got it, and if you change your mind about waiting to change the title just let me know."

Jacob was momentarily buffaloed. He had not actually expected Harvey to agree.

"You brought Robert out for me, even though he was too injured to live. You gave him back to me and I was able to talk with him before he died. That meant everything to me. He was the love of my life. There will never be another like Robert."

Jacob couldn't believe what he was hearing. Tears were rolling down the big man's cheeks. He didn't appreciate Harvey's lifestyle, but the emotion was universal.

"You didn't know about me, did you Jacob?"

"No! But your sex life is not my concern, Harvey. It's all I can do to keep up with my own. What consenting adults do is no business of mine."

Back at Harvey's office they signed the papers selling the property to a company Jacob had set up: RBI Construction Company. Harvey's secretary witnessed signatures, Harvey handed Jacob the ring of keys and he headed back to his office.

Johnny was still there, but Mary had left. "Johnny, we need to get someone to guard Mary. We can't be with her all the time, since we both have businesses to run. Do you know anyone we can trust?"

"D.R., I'm in love."

"That quick, huh?"

"The minute she walked in you could have hit me with a baseball bat and I wouldn't have noticed."

"Congratulations! Let's hope the lady feels the same, although no reason she shouldn't be attracted to such a handsome, muscular wart hog like you."

"We'll have to step high to get through the shit around here," Irish said, grinning like a kid caught skinny-dipping. "Dammit, D.R., don't kid me, this is serious. I intend to marry her if I can convince her what a swell catch I am."

"Now who's stepping high? It's okay, Johnny, I do understand and will give you all the time you need here to convince her. Back now to the original question: Who can we get to guard her?"

"Other than you or Dozer, the only other man I know would be Jason Devin. He worked a lot with Dozer, Boom and me, but never made the readjustment when we returned. He's been in and out of jail, but nothing really bad. Some smart asses thought he would be an easy rip-off. I'll see if he's at his last place."

It was three p.m. when Johnny returned with a man who looked like he had just come from a run in the jungle. Vietnam was still written all over him. He was obviously still at war, wearing camouflage utilities and lace-up boots. His hair was thin at the crown, but long and pulled back in a neat ponytail, and his facial hair was neatly sculpted into a gray Jesus beard.

"Do you need any equipment?" Jacob asked.

"Yeah! I could use a gun. Any kind will do. I've got everything else I need in the car."

"Let's go outside. I have a couple of guns in the trunk of my car. You can take your pick." Jacob had three of the shooter's guns; one was a Glock .40-caliber, loaded with jacketed hollow-points. He figured that would be the one Jason would choose, but instead, he chose a .38 Special, explaining: "I can hit anything with this—grew up shooting one."

"Johnny has already filled me in and we stopped to get what I need. Skipper, I appreciate this chance and I won't let you down."

"Glad to have you on board, Jason. Since you have your own car, you follow Johnny and he can stay to help you set up. I'd go but I'm expecting some important information to be hand delivered sometime before five. Take this phone, I have another. The red button is my home and the blue one is this office. The green is police and they are all direct dial. Johnny briefed you, didn't he?"

"Yeah! He told me what happened. How the hell did you happen to be there?"

"I still work out in those woods across from her house. Just happened on the action. It wasn't deliberate."

"Son of a gun . . . another one of your dead reckonings? Don't worry, Skipper. I'll get them if they show up."

"I know you will, Jason." There was no hesitation in his voice. Jason had proven himself to Boom's, Johnny's and Bulldozer's satisfaction.

A car pulled in the parking lot as Jacob watched Johnny and Jason leave. It came to a screeching halt just feet in front of him and a grinning, bubbly Inez jumped out, all four-feet-four inches of perfect womanhood. Her husband, Joe, had to strap blocks to the car pedals so she could see to drive sitting on a pillow.

"Got what you wanted by taking a late lunch. You said you needed it yesterday. I drew you a map; it's in the envelope with the truck papers and tag. The truck will be ready Tuesday. They're painting it dark blue. Already had the paint. Joe said to call him if you can use him anytime. It seems you've started a tremble in the jungle. They all know there's no way you will take your disbarment sitting down. Yeah! I almost forgot, you need to give me eight hundred and fifty-three dollars for insurance, tag, etc. I paid the insurance for a year."

"Great job, tidbit. I owe you."

She just grinned and held out her hand. He pulled out his wallet and handed her fifteen hundred. "Don't have any change, take Joe out to dinner. Now scat so I can get on the road. Things are a-happening."

"Joe will be glad to hear it. He said he wants to help."

"Joe always said you hung the moon, now I believe him."

"You just don't know what he really meant by that! And, don't ask! Bye!"

She jumped in the car, turned around and sped off down the street. Big Joe was six-feet-two, 240 pounds of solid muscle. Jacob didn't try to figure that one out.

Chapter 9

Built as part of an old brick mill complex, the warehouse looked from the outside much like any other; that resemblance, however, ended at the door. The 120- by 40-foot upstairs room had been divided into two bedrooms, two baths, a closet and a great room-kitchen combination separated by a long counter with stools. The heavy floorboards were sanded smooth and stained a faded denim blue. Jacob had added a skylight, new windows, doors and a pipe fireman's ladder to an enclosure within the warehouse in addition to the stairs that came down between the two offices.

Joe Monroe had spray painted the inside of the building an off-white color, spraying everything in sight, including ceiling, walls, and pipes. Afterwards Irish and his buddies had divided the last bay in the warehouse into three rooms: a workout area with hot tub, a bunkroom with bath and a kitchen with picnic tables outside and in. Now they had their own private club. Privacy fences went up on either side and back to the woods. Hidden gates all around corresponded with steel mesh driveways through the woods covered with mulch. A bunch of old guys together again who understood war and were contemplating the disasters threatening their peaceful existence.

The old warehouse had once been used by a construction company that had gone bankrupt, with all the equipment auctioned off except one rusty old backhoe. Bulldozer was methodically restoring it to its former glory.

D.R., Irish and Jason had been alternating at night in the hutch across from Mary's house. Tonight, D.R. took his watch at one a.m., wearing his usual camouflage coveralls and cloak. He settled down in the foliage of a scrub oak thicket and waited. At four a.m. he yawned, needing to move his cramped legs and relieve himself.

Just when he decided it was safe and started to move, a shadow flashed across his peripheral vision. He froze in a semi-crouched position. Then the shadow moved again, toward the back of Mary's house. D.R. watched the carefully moving figure gain the house and move alongside, disappearing behind the house. D.R. moved fast because there was no time to move in his usual careful manner. Even now he feared he would be too late.

With his back against the house, he peered around the back corner, expecting to see the man working on a window or door. Suddenly he realized no one was there. Turning defensively, he saw the knife slicing toward him. His hand automatically struck out to dislodge the knife and he felt the bone of his assailant break. With his right hand he threw a gut punch with all his might and fell to the side, throwing the attacker over his hip. The man grunted when he hit the ground but continued to roll, getting instantly to his feet. He shoved his broken arm into a slit pocket in his jacket. This man was a professional, otherwise he would have been screaming. Instead, he was absorbing the pain and coming back at D.R., with a gun he had taken from a side pocket of his utilities. Jerking at his weapon, D.R. threw himself to one side, firing as he fell. He felt a hammer blow to his shoulder. Adrenaline pumping, he rolled behind some landscape timbers lining a flowerbed. He waited. The man didn't move, but it could be a trick. D.R. pulled his cell phone from his pocket and punched in Irish's number. That was all he had to do; Irish would be there quickly.

His left arm not responding as usual, he opened and closed his fingers, finding that with effort he could move it. Crawling slowly around the timbers, he approached the man's head. The assailant still held the gun, pointed now to the left of his feet. Holding heat sensor goggles to his eyes, D.R. could tell the man wasn't dead, only wounded in the side. He was playing possum. D.R. did not want to kill him. This time the police would be involved and he didn't want to be cited for murder. He spoke softly, "Drop the gun or die!"

"Okay! Don't shoot!"

The gun fell from the assailant's hand and he pushed it away with a sweep of his arm. Then he rolled suddenly, pulling another gun faster than D.R. thought possible. Fire raced across D.R.'s ribs as he rolled, shooting at the moving figure as another bullet screamed past his ear. Numbness and then a burning pain slid into his consciousness. He was hit and losing blood. It rolled down inside his coveralls from two wounds. He listened for movement and heard nothing. Crawling around to a pecan tree, he pulled himself up by holding onto the low growing limbs. The security light shone on the man on the ground. Blood seeped from a wound midway from his shoulder to his waist and a dark dot of red was in the middle of his forehead. What the shit! D.R. knew he had not made a head shot. Yet, there was the dark bloody spot. Another trick? He felt as if clouds were filling the space in front of his eyes and he blinked to see better, when the man on the ground suddenly lifted his gun. The loud report of a .45 made the fake bloody hole in the assassin's forehead a reality.

"D.R.? Cool it man, he won't ever play dead again."

"Irish, I want to know who that sucker was. He just kept coming. I didn't want to kill him, I wanted him to talk!"

"D.R., if you're able, you need to leave. I was already here and tangled with him, since it was my shot that finished him. I have a reason to be here. We'll talk later. Give me your gun."

"No! It can be traced to the first assassin. I need to know who this man was."

"I'll go through his pockets. Move man!"

Lights came on in the house.

"Mary is calling the police now. I told her to call if she heard gunfire and mine was the only shot she heard."

"All right! I'll meet you back at the warehouse."

Keeping to the shadows, fighting waves of weakness washing over him, D.R. slowly made his way back toward his truck. Blood was soaking his utilities and he hoped it wasn't dripping. Picking up his cloaking tent, he held it to his body and made his way through the woods thinking he must have parked farther than he remembered. Clawing the door to the truck open, unable to raise his arm, he pushed himself into the truck, then with his good right arm he settled himself behind the wheel and started the engine. Driving like a drunken sailor, taking shortcuts through fields, yards and flowerbeds, he made it to the warehouse, thinking he would call Sarah to come and doctor his wounds. Punching the garage door opener he drove into the first bay, stumbled from the truck and went to the bunkroom. Jason was there and got up when D.R. came in.

"Good lord! Vesuvius is erupting out of your shoulder, D.R.! Sit here let me stop that bleeding!"

All D.R. could get out was, "Call Sarah!" He took two more steps and collapsed on a bunk.

The hum of an idling backhoe woke him and he slowly opened his eyes to see a halo around a blonde head. His first thought was that he was dead and this was an angel. Then he realized as his sight cleared that it was Sarah sitting in a rocking chair beside the bunk with a novel propped up on her knees, her feet resting on a metal stool. His mouth was desert dry.

"Sa—Sarah?"

"Well, D.R., welcome back to the land of the living."

"I thought you were an angel."

"You almost made the jump this time friend. One inch farther to the left and you would have been seeing real angels. It's been a while since I did any fine darning, so I called Dr. Harry to come down. Even so, that little shoulder wound took all his talents. What kind of bullets was that rat slinging?"

"I didn't take time to ask. Did it do any permanent damage?"

"Not that Harry could tell, but it will take time to heal. Harry worked on it for four hours with a magnifying glass. It only took twenty stitches to pull that furrow in your side together. That was a smaller caliber bullet and it will be well in no time. I gave you a booster tetanus, vitamin K, a B-12 and antibiotics. Harry said to tell you no moving that arm. That's why it's taped to your chest. And you are to leave it there or lose the use of it permanently. Comprehend compadre?"

"Yeah! You're scaring me out of my drawers, except I don't seem to have any on. Where's Irish?"

"Two guesses and the second guess doesn't count."

"He's with Mary."

"Give the man a red balloon! Bulldozer wants to talk with you. I'll get him. Mary and Irish have answered questions for three different law enforcement agencies. I sent them to my house. Irish said tell you he had news and would see you tomorrow. I gave you a sedative a few minutes before you woke up, knowing you would think you're invincible. Jason and I will be here and Bulldozer and the other guys won't let anyone in here. Sleep baby, sleep and heal. Harry said next time for you to shoot faster and straighter. His back is killing him from bending over for so long."

Sarah kept him drugged out for two days. He was sitting up drinking some broth when Bulldozer came in.

"Irish explained the *problem* and if it's okay with you, I'd like to help out. Looks like you need a little R&R for the moment. Irish and Boom gave me a poke full of money, so I'm getting some more equipment and starting us a business. That money has to come from somewhere. Irish said you already have a business license and the warehouse in the name of RBI Construction, so we'll just use that if it's okay with you. Of course we could change it to RBBI but the B can stand for Boom and Bulldozer. Just one thing, any action you engage in the future, I'd appreciate it if you would let me in on the fun!"

"Last trip wasn't much fun, Bulldozer. You need to know this is a much more evil machine than I at first realized. Guess I was a bit rusty. Thought I had left the killing behind me."

"Hell man, you're fifty-two and that sucker was thirty-three and a trained assassin. Of course, I could've taken him with the first shot, but you—you didn't want to kill him and to kill him was the only way. I've looked into this a bit and it will be more subtle in some ways than the jungle, but it's still the jungle, just a little harder to discern the enemy. Has Mary said who's after her?"

"I haven't talked with Irish yet. Has he told you anything?"

"He was waiting for you to wake up and help him convince her. You'll have to tell her about the first one, then she'll be able to see they really mean to kill her."

"I will have to tell her the whole story if Irish can't get her to talk. Think about it . . . you can run the business, you don't need to get involved in our problems. You have five boys and a wife to think of first. I think there's a connection between Mary's bad guys and the ones who are after me. Only mine just want to destroy me one piece at a time, not kill me—at least not yet."

"D.R., the only dude in a three piece suit I want to work for is myself. I fully intend to run a profitable grading company. You know I only take orders from Zelda." He looked down and grinned. "She's a tough boss. Those boys snap-to when she talks and she's a whiz at books. I can do the fieldwork and you just handle any legal shit. How much was in that stash anyway?"

"We don't know, didn't bother to count it."

"That much, huh?"

"Enough that you don't have to ever worry about your mortgage again. Take the second bay for your equipment. Whoever is here can answer for us. You just tell me what you want me to do. Zelda can talk with Inez to get any permits."

D.R. was pleased to be working with Bulldozer. The Dozer was a legend, a hero beyond any he had ever known. Stories about him were abundant. Every pilot he rode with had one to tell. He was the first to jump from the Huey to lift wounded onto the deck. Finding Marines where they had hidden in the jungle, surrounded by the enemy, he had snatched them from under the noses of the VC, carrying them, hiding them for however long it took to get them out. Bulldozer Bush was a complex, intelligent, strong man who had great compassion and deadly accuracy. D.R. knew, for he had once marched with the man.

The only survivor of a Huey crash, he had wandered the jungle for three weeks before finding his way back to base. Some said his being lost was because he didn't want to be found. Several grunt platoons had run into a man fitting his description who asked for supplies, but he had refused to return with them. He had a score to settle and when he did come back he brought five men with him who had been *detained* by the VC.

Mary and Irish were waiting when D.R. awoke late the next day. Irish was telling Bulldozer that after the police took the man's fingerprints and determined his identity they didn't even notice he was shot with two different guns. Irish was the admitted shooter so the bullets were not removed. "The killer's name was Fob Nelson, commonly known as The Fish Fob. The police had been after him for years, afraid they would catch up to him. Three who had were dead. They were grateful to me for putting him permanently out of circulation."

"Thank God for that. With all my other trouble, killing a guy would've gotten me maxed out in every newspaper. What do I have to do to get some service in here? Where the hell is the coffee that's driving my taste buds crazy?"

"Oh! So you finally want to get your lazy ass off the bed, do you? Come on Bulldozer, we'll throw him out the window."

"Just remember I still have one good arm!"

"You just remember that one good arm is attached to the muscles in your side and there are about twenty stitches holding your side together!"

Irish swung him up so he could slide his legs over the side of the bed. "When are you going to ask that girl to marry you?" He had said it to cover the dizziness he was feeling. His brain felt like mush rolling around in his head. Irish blushed. "I'm going to sit here until you do."

Mary walked over and put her arms around Irish. "Say yes, Johnny!"

"Yes!" Johnny pulled Mary close and gave her a quick kiss, looking at her as man has since time began.

D.R. said, "Now that we have that settled will one of you hysterically happy people fix me some breakfast?"

Sitting around the table eating scrambled eggs, bacon and grits, they began to fill in the story. "The police found money on the shooter — a lot of money — and were ecstatic. It will go into their police retirement fund," Irish explained.

"Mary, now that you are engaged and know we can be trusted, will you please tell us who is trying to kill you and why," D.R. said. "You have to tell me what you know. Is it Bubba? What do you know that is scaring some very rich men so much that they are hiring shooters?"

"How do you know this wasn't just an isolated attack?" she asked.

"Because this is the second attack on your life," D.R. said.

The blood drained from her face. "Why . . . when? Surely they wouldn't — they couldn't. How do you know? You said the second? When was the first?"

"On October thirtieth. You got home about seven-fifteen. You were wearing a green coat and short boots and carrying groceries into your house. A man was waiting behind the kudzu with a rifle. I was working-out in the woods and stopped him only a second before he pulled the trigger."

"My God! I remember that night. I felt like someone

had walked over my grave."

"It was close, very close. Do you think Bubba is hiring these shooters?"

"No! Not him. It could be a client of his, though. My research was a bit too thorough." She had been pouring coffee refills; now she reached for the arm of a chair and eased herself down, her knees weak from the sudden realization that two men had been sent to kill her and both were dead!

"What did you see or discover? So far two men have died trying to kill you, and one was injured trying to save you," D.R. said. "The next assassin could succeed. To keep you alive, we need to know everything you know. It was close. If I hadn't been there that night, Mary, we would not be having this conversation. Papers in his car showed that he was a hired assassin. Since we don't know who is involved, you must not talk to anyone but Irish, Bulldozer, Boom or myself. Whoever is after you has hired this second killer since the first failed. That's a lot of money, Mary. You've got someone very important very scared and when men like that are scared they don't stop."

Mary's face turned white and she almost fainted. Irish draped his arm around her shoulders. She grabbed for her coffee and took a sip then looked right at D.R.. "You lied to Maurice. I talked with him and he said you mentioned my name first. You lied to me. How do I know I can trust you?"

"Yes, I lied to you—but for a reason. Did you expect me to approach a woman I didn't know and tell her an assassin had tried to kill her? You would've thought me a crazy idiot. Therefore, the next day, after the first attempt, I called a friend at voter registration and got the name at your address, your phone number and where you worked. When Maurice came in, I played my little lie in order to pull you in to protect you. Now you know all that I know! Your turn to talk."

She was sitting there with her mouth open. The full realization a minute earlier opened her eyes as round as a

Raggedy Ann's and her mouth formed a beautiful circle of horrified surprise. It came out in a tiny whisper. "You killed him?"

"I didn't say that. I just said he didn't get close enough to kill you. Which would you rather it have been? Him or you? I didn't feel you deserved the punishment he was about to inflict. He was a paid professional, had been killing people for profit for over thirty years. Mary, there are many different kinds of war. I think Irish can explain this to your satisfaction. Fortunately for you someone was there to help. Others haven't been so lucky. I could not be with you all the time and neither could Irish, so we hired Jason and the three of us have been guarding your house every time you leave the office. It was fortunate that Irish was at your house the last time. But you can't tell the police, Mary. They were grateful to Irish because that man had killed other policemen. This isn't a tea party you've gotten yourself involved in and if we are to help you, we have to know everything."

She took a deep breath; tears formed and ran down her cheeks. "You did that for me? For someone you didn't even know?"

"We're all warriors and so is Jason. We're trained to protect those who cannot protect themselves. Warriors don't cease to be what they are just because they are retired. Irish and I reacted instinctively to a cold blooded attempt at murder."

She wiped her eyes with a napkin and blew her nose. Two men were dead because of something she knew, and D.R. was shot up; it was unbelievable. Suddenly she could hold back no longer. All the fear, days and nights of constant fear and worry. But should she bring these men into it any further? They were already deeply involved and she realized she had no choice. "A contractor that Bubba represents . . . builds motels around the country . . . he puts what he calls service corridors in the walls, but what it is really for is to put peepholes in all the rooms. While researching his file I found plans that clearly showed the corridors. That in itself was incriminating, until I found out he was photographing and blackmailing people.

"Further research showed legal work billed to people in parts of the country where the firm is not licensed to work. The billings were done by Edgar Walsh. The person who did the supposed *consulting* was Critcher Linebarger. I looked those names up and found hours of consulting done for them, that I know was never done. There were no expense vouchers to back up any trips or lunches or secretarial time. Men sometimes think we are invisible and talk around us, thinking they are being clever, when someone working like I do can take snatches and find the whole picture.

"In all innocence I told Bubba that I thought that was a horrible thing to do, spying on people. Later, in the library I had dropped a book behind a desk. It fell open to the page I wanted and I sat down on the floor to copy the short paragraph. Bubba and a friend of his, Phil Williams, came into the library. It looked empty and it was late; I should have already left. Phil Williams owns several real estate companies. He hires young beautiful girls and sends them on seminars to exotic places. He asked Bubba to join him at a seminar in Hawaii. 'The Girls will be wonderful, you will enjoy yourself,' he said.

"To Bubba's credit, he said 'You're crazy Phil, they will talk.' Whereupon Phil replied, 'No they won't. We drug them and they never know a thing. You know, I have three children now and they don't even know they are mine! It's the greatest high in the world! You've got to try it!' I was shocked to stillness by what I heard. I wanted to scream at them, to throw things, but I kept perfectly still. They laughed some more and mentioned meeting their wives at the club, then they walked out. I waited ten minutes without moving a muscle. Then I got out of there as fast as I could. The next morning, Joe Martin, the office manager, asked me why I signed out so late and where was I working. I told him in the basement. But I don't think he believed me. A week later I was fired.

"Fifteen years, I've been a paralegal and never realized anything this abusive could be going on under my nose. I feel like a fool. Premeditated rape and pregnancy by men of supposed distinction? Dear God! They're awful. I know some of the girls who went on those trips. It's horrible! What they are doing is so wrong! Instead of stopping, they're trying to murder me!"

"Irish, she had better stay here for now," D.R. said. "We'll all look after you, Mary. They won't be able to find Mrs. Johnny Michaels if there are no records. Now you try to relax and get those dark circles out from under those pretty eyes. You're safe. Believe me, nobody will bother you but Johnny, okay?"

"Okay!" The tears were falling now. D.R. patted her hand. "We'll get this straightened out, don't worry."

D.R. wasn't really surprised by Mary's revelations about Williams. He had known for a long time about the motel corridors. That's why the RV market had boomed in the eighties. It was something no one talked about but most people suspected. It was the drugging and rape of employees that Williams didn't want to get out. It would put him in jail and ruin his financial affairs. Phil or his buddies could unknowingly be spreading venereal infections to innocent people, not to mention the emotional and religious aspects of their evil acts. What they were doing was exceedingly criminal — man in his lowest animal form.

It was beyond going to the police. Not only would it ruin Mary's life, but also it would ruin all the young women involved, and in spite of their innocence, their reputations. Most people considered the innocent guilty in some way when they were abused, as in "She must have done something wrong for something like that to happen to her." Or the whispers following the children, "You know who his father really is? It was a big scandal." D.R. could hear the wagging tongues following all the people involved for a lifetime. He did not want that to happen to such innocent victims.

Damn! I would never have thought Williams would jeopardize his reputation, his career in such a manner. A pillar of the community, a deacon at his Church, he's on the board of directors at the home for unwed mothers for Christ's sake, he must have put a few there. Williams, in addition to others, you just fucked up your life when you sent those men after Mary. The thought of Phil Williams sweating Mary's disappearance brought a smile.

"What are you finding to smile about?" Mary asked.

"Just at how worried Phil will be when he can't find you, Mary."

"Murder isn't funny!" she replied, anger in her voice.

"No it isn't, Mary, but sometimes getting back can be a fun game among men. Don't you like to see the bad guy get his comeuppance?"

"Well, I suppose so—but it's much more enjoyable on TV than in real life."

"Welcome to the real world, Mary."

Chapter 10

Hot metal fragments riddled Willis' body, severing his jugular. His buddies scrambled forward only to see Willis on his side supported by thick brush, his face white, eyes empty and staring into space. Blood flowed out over his ripped shirt collar, flooding in a deadly stream down his jacket to drip on the powdery forest mulch.

Miller frantically tried to stem the flow of blood with his hand, but he was already too late. Grasping Miller's shoulder, Captain Anderson pointed to a large metal fragment protruding from Willis' temple. Both men realized that Willis was beyond help. Tears found purchase between the red welts of mosquito bites on Miller's face, sliding freely down the tanned cheeks of the warrior, who with a tight lower lip swallowed sobs of grief. With reverence, he effectively collected the remains of Corporal Willis and placed him in a green plastic zippered bag. Where Willis had bled on the forest mulch, Miller gathered the bloodstained mulch, putting it in the bag, not wanting to leave even one drop of Willis' blood on the alien soil.

In grief stricken rage, Miller streaked his face with his bloodstained hands, then crawled through the thick brush, checking for more mines as he progressed. He pulled Willis' body behind him, remembering the day Willis had saved his life by yanking him back when his foot was only an inch from stepping on a mine.

Anderson swallowed around the knot in his throat, refusing to give in to the horror of loss. He had to keep going, to get the other three men safely back. Now on his belly with the damp musty smell of forest mulch up his nose, bugs crawling across his hands and arms and gnats using his eyes for a landing field, he suppressed a sneeze and the horrible, almost uncontrollable urge to swat. Taking a handful of snuff-like mulch from under his nose, he squeezed his fist and water rolled over his hand. Two of his men were in prone positions on either side of him, listening to the deadly, humming vibration of the North Vietnamese Army searching methodically through the brush. When he was fourteen, hiking through deep woods, Anderson had found a rotting pile of old wood and poked it with his hiking stick. Pulling the dead wood aside, he had seen and heard the vibrating hum of the exposed termites eating the rotting wood. That sound came back to him now, listening to the deadly humming vibration of the NVA. "Too many, must be a battalion!" Anderson spoke quietly over his shoulder while crawling toward a rocky opening in the forest canopy. A tiny hint of a spring ran through the middle of a large creek bed.

Lee Jones crawled up beside him. "What do we do now, Cap'n?"

"Let's get the hell out of here, Lee."

"I'm afraid that's impossible; we're surrounded. They're everywhere! We're cut off south and west, so there's no going back. East is the cliff, a sheer drop of approximately five hundred feet. North is that wide-open stony ridge. Looks like we got on a parallel trail to the one we were supposed to recon. Nothing on the map like this."

The knowing fear in the young Marine's eyes only mirrored Anderson's own. They were trapped like rabbits by the North Vietnamese Army. Now, Anderson could even smell them. The survival unit was in his hand and he set the intermittent signal. He knew the rules, had taken the risk. The President and the Secretary of State would deny having any troops in the area. Hell! The North Vietnamese Army wasn't supposed to be here either! It didn't matter; there would be no medals, no recognition—just a *missing in action* to the families of the men involved. He was a Marine, but he had no death wish. Damned if he would take a dirt nap without at least trying.

Two CH-46 pilots flying back from a resupply mission just across the border received the signal. Lead pilot Reynolds instructed his wingman to orbit and locate the beacon. Flying across a spiny ridge that would give new meaning to razorback, they spotted the recon team down near the rocky ridge. Now they could see the surrounding enemy.

"God almighty, damn! Will you look at that! Looks like a stirred up hill of fire ants! Holy schmoley, it's a fucking battalion! Ready up guys! We're going in."

Coming in fast and low they unwittingly drew fire on the recon team's position. Making a tight turn, they came down again, setting the aircraft down lengthwise on the spine with the ramp of the aircraft partially open. They saw a uniformed enemy soldier stand up to throw a grenade at the crouching, running men. Logan Turner, manning the .50 caliber machine gun on the copilots side, took the thrower out, but the grenade was already in the air. It fell short, but some fragments reached the running men, who, momentarily stunned, continued in a stumbling gait toward the backing helicopter. Turner's gun jammed and he switched to the crew chief's weapon. The crew chief moved to the rear door of the aircraft to assist and direct the backing maneuvers down the spine toward the recon team. Reynolds held the brakes and looked back down the length of the fuselage.

Three of the recon team made it to the plane. Anderson shouted for Miller and frantically searched the area for some sign of him. He saw nothing and there was no answer to his yelling. Returning fire, they hit top speed out of there heading for Khe Sahn. Glancing back, Reynolds was horrified to see one they missed. He was holed up just below the top of the cliff. Reynolds watched as the Marine, crouched in a hole on the side of the cliff face, tried desperately to hold onto a body bag. He freed one hand to wave the helicopter away and in doing so the bag slipped from his grasp and slid down the cliff face. Reynolds knew the Marine was trying to keep his buddy out of the hands of the Vietnam Regulars, and hoped they did not see the body fall. Directly above the Marine, hundreds of uniformed soldiers were setting up antiaircraft weapons.

Calling for close air support and another chopper mission, Reynolds reported that the crew had severe casualties and requested medical evacuation. Radio traffic began to sound like the Santa Monica freeway. Reynolds' mind kept bringing up a picture of the anguish on the Marine's face as the body bag had slipped from his hands. There was no way they could get to him with hundreds of the enemy swarming on the rock directly above his head. Under his breath he said, "Just hold on man, I'll be back to get you."

Chapter 11

How could he get out of the country without leaving a significant paper trail? Perhaps he could drive to Watertown, New York, then take a bus or train into Canada. From there he could fly to Mexico City and then on to Dublin where he could take the ferry to England, then the hydrofoil to France. He wondered how quickly they would be able to put that all together should flight ever become necessary. Anyway, it was best to have a plan, especially with what he had in mind. He didn't have to worry about running out of money; it was stashed away in several easily accessible places.

The immediate problem was keeping Mary safe, which was being worked out, with Irish doing most of the watching. Jacob was damned happy for his friend. Irish deserved a good woman who would love him without trying to change him — at least not too much.

At Marty's restaurant on the square that morning, Jacob had talked with Hiram Weis. Hiram was defending Jack Murdock, accused of mutilating and killing two local women. When Hiram had said there was not enough evidence to convict his client, Jacob felt fury well up within himself. Hiram could not compromise his client because of attorney-client privilege, but he did say: "I hate defending this kind of thing. Whether or not the guy's guilty, he will walk. The prosecution just can't prove its case unless they come up with something new. All they have is circumstantial evidence."

Right then, Jacob had decided to investigate and find

out for sure whether Murdock was guilty. A flash of Mary and what would have happened to her had he not taken that workout in the woods at that particular time made him shudder. Maybe he was developing a hero complex, he didn't know, but he did know that if Jack Murdock walked, he would not go free. What was done to those women proved the killer was no longer human, which made him fair game for any man.

After coming back home from Vietnam, Jacob had seen enough violence done to women and children that it was just too much for him to take. Why did good people put up with that kind of abuse and not rise up in mass and stone the perpetrators? Besides kicking women and poking them to death with a stick, the only other thing Jack Murdock seemed to like was drinking at Toby's bar at least five days a week.

It was Jacob's alter ego, D.R., who walked into Toby's bar Saturday night and ordered a double scotch. At the end of the long oak bar, Jack Murdock was talking quietly to his sidekick, Buck Rowen, a weak-backed, sallow-faced gambling buddy. Like all drunks, his whispering was much louder than he realized. Willie Nelson provided a loud backdrop from the jukebox when D.R. walked behind the two men to get to the men's room. He then turned quickly and walked silently back just in time to hear Jack whisper to his buddy, "Hell, yes, I did it! But, I won't spend a day in jail! Buck, you should've seen old Morris' face when he heard what was done to his wife; he was all broke up. I had to try hard to keep from laughing. If he gets too loose with his money and lawyers, I'll just have to see that he has an accident."

Having heard all he needed to hear, Jacob turned to go back to the men's room when he sensed rather than saw, in a dark corner behind the men, his friend, Bulldozer. He was sitting in a chair, a small electronic unit in his hand with a plug in his ear. He motioned Jacob off with a hand signal.

Puzzled, Jacob paid for his drinks and left. Outside

standing beside his Rover was Irish. "What's happening, buddy?"

"Man, I'm hungry. Let's go over to the Waffle House and get some breakfast."

They took a booth, ordered coffee and looked at the menu. "Looks like we need to coordinate our action," Irish said. "Betty's husband asked our friend to find out if Jack killed Betty. He also told him what the killer had done to Betty and her friend. This is his move, he hopes you won't mind. Dozer didn't realize what you were up to until about twenty minutes ago. He kept waiting for you to leave. Then he called me to pick you up outside and give you the message."

Back at Toby's, Bulldozer waited for the cook to turn his back, then slipped out the kitchen door. He saw Murdock get into his shiny new red Camaro. "You might drive away sicko, but you won't get away."

"Irish, I still can't figure how some men think they are so tough, beating up on women. That man doesn't know tough. He's never messed with tough. But he will know soon — very soon." Jacob remembered the last time he had seen Betty. She and her daughter, Amy, had been in the courthouse looking up records of land transactions. Amy was getting married and Betty was buying her a lot for a house as her wedding present. Betty never got to see the wedding. She and another woman had picnicked in the park to plan the wedding and both had been killed by one inhuman monster.

"Tis a foggy night for the law me frien' D.R., but methinks the air will be clearer by morning." Irish laughed.

"Who's watching Mary?"

"She's with Zelda."

"I'd ask you if you're sure nobody followed you, but my head is already foolish enough as it is."

"What are you going to eat?"

"I want one of those everything omelets and everything hash browns and a barrel of coffee."

The souped up Camaro roared into the garage, which was separate from the Murdock's old family home. Jack Murdock took a drink out of his bottle, carefully capped it and put it on the floor of the car. Then he opened the door. As he got out, he saw a shadowy figure in the doorway. "What the hell!" He didn't have time to say anything else as the *shadow* took two steps and hit him in the stomach. He fell against the wall of the garage and got up in a crouch, trying to see who had hit him.

"Look buddy, if you want the car just take it, please don't hit me again." While he was talking he pulled a gun from the back band of his jeans, but before he could get a grip to fire, it was plucked from his hand like taking candy from a baby. He grabbed a shovel from a wall bracket, only to receive a blow to his face, and then the shovel was wrenched from his grasp. Murdock took a wild swing and hit solid muscle. The next instant the sharp blade of the shovel was thrust into his groin.

"This is for the women you killed."

Murdock tried to yell, but no sound came forth. His tormentor was dragging him out of the garage only to drop him past the row of Baby's Breath lining the driveway. He tried to crawl away, but his groin muscles would not work. He was begging in a rasping whisper for mercy, hoping the man would now leave him alone.

A knife ripped his jeans and he thought, "My God! He's going to rape me." But he soon found out differently as the cold blades of a pair of pruning shears were viciously thrust into place. A vision of the women he had killed flashed through his mind. The scream never left his lips but was mirrored on his face.

A heavy boot kicked the long blades farther, and then strong muscular arms picked Murdock up and turned him over, a sharp knife in his big fist. "Trash, you're not worth the effort." He returned the knife to his boot, picked up the shovel and with a mighty thrust pinned the man to the ground.

With gloved hands he then picked up a rag and wiped the car clean. He didn't want Mrs. Murdock to find her nephew dead, or to have to clean up the mess, nor did he want to leave any prints.

Back behind the warehouse, Bulldozer stripped off his clothes and stood naked in the cold night air. He soaked the boots with gasoline and threw them into the smoldering trash barrel. D.R. made a lot of noise coming out the door, handed him a robe and a glass of brandy. The Dozer was shaking. D.R. didn't know if it was from the cold or from anger and horror at his own actions. For the first time, he noticed the road map of scars on the big man's body. Not once during the war had he ever known Bulldozer to complain of injury. He was surprised at what the big man now said:

"Dammit, D.R.! I didn't need backup to take care of that pile of rags."

"Yeah, I hope it was neat and satisfying with a lot of prolonged pain. Maybe if there are any other sicko's like Murdock out there they will get the message."

"They never seem to get the message, D.R. You know that!" He filled a can with gasoline and chucked it in the barrel, then tossed in a match. The barrel exploded in a mass of flames shooting high into the air. Got another cleanup job to do tomorrow night. There's a pharmacist south out of Atlanta who is into child porn. I want to take care of that scum but I'm turning over the information to Todd Andrews; he's with the Agency. He asked me to come along with them to pick up the sick fucker. I'd rather take care of it myself, but in this case he needs the publicity. If it were left to me I'd take Doc and give him a split message. If he gets out anytime soon, I will."

D.R. winced at the thought, slapped Dozer on the back, and said, "Need any help?"

"No! You're too high profiled just now. I'm willing to bet you'll be questioned about Murdock's death. They know about you, but nobody here except you guys know me."

"Dozer, how do you cope with the nightmares?"

"Don't have any — never have. Always have had a feeling of rightness in what I do. I don't go out killing needlessly. War was to me a coming together of what I was born to do. A woman once told me her son was born knowing how to swim. I was born to be a warrior — it happens. I do what needs to be done. I must have a little knight errant tucked away somewhere in my psyche — probably a hero complex. Wanting to protect the innocent so that the fair maidens will shower my brow with kisses. You know, all that stuff that good men are scared to do. You know that *something* put you at Mary's at the right time to save her life. That same thing guides me. Although some would say it's evil, I think of it as justice."

"You're right."

"People don't report abuse because of the stupidity of other people and the vicious gossips who have no understanding of innocence attacked. A lot of men abuse their children, and the mother never reports it. She thinks she is protecting the reputation of the family or the child. Zelda has been telling me about this. She's giving some time to the abuse center. She's upset that the abused women don't realize they are abetting the abuser by leaving him free to abuse other children. Does that make her a party to the abuse? Not only of her children, but the others as well? Some women are just too weak to respond, but there are those who know and do nothing, through fear of being homeless, I guess.

"D.R., it might surprise you that I go to church every Sunday. I think there is great beauty in the principle of religion and if it worked there would be no need for men like me. No child deserves some sex deviate working out fantasies on them. Why should I lose sleep because I eliminated a predator of the innocent?"

"You're right, Dozer. It's simple; some people just make it complicated. Looks like I've been wasting sleep on nightmares I don't deserve. God! We're wonderful fuck-ups aren't we?"

"The best!"

"Come on, let's try out that new hot tub the guys put in." The Dozer was out of the dark rage, back into the light. In the distance, streak lightning split the sky. Bulldozer looked up and said, "Going to rain good tonight." He filled another tin can with gasoline and threw it in the barrel. "Picked those boots up at a yard sale, never did fit." He picked up his utilities and went inside. "Okay! Let's soak out the kinks."

It was just after three the next day when the sheriff walked into the warehouse. Seeing everyone busy, he asked the man nearest the door where he could find Jacob Reynolds.

Irish pointed to the office.

Jacob was on the phone. "Hi! Sam, have a seat. I'll be off the phone in a minute . . . Let me call you later, I need to do some research on this before I answer. I put on a doozy last night and the cobwebs are just popping." He laughed and put down the phone.

"Well Sam, how do you like my new place?"

"Damndest thing I ever saw! What are you starting? A spa garage?"

"Kinda looks that way doesn't it." Jacob laughed and continued, "I rent office space from the construction company of which I have half interest, which you probably already know. They have the rest of the place. Did you come over to be sure I'm not practicing law?"

"No! Got something else on my mind. You hear about Jack Murdock?"

"Hell yes! That ran like wildfire through town this morning. I was at Marty's for his famous hangover cure-all when George Morgan — Mrs. Murdock's yard man — ran in screaming. Do you think one of the husbands did it?"

"Well, Shorty Lee said you were there last night and left just before Murdock did. Said you looked pretty drunk."

"You got the drunk part right. Johnny Irish met me outside the bar and we went to the Waffle House for breakfast. He brought me home. Don't think I could have made it without him."

"What time did you get home?"

"Damn, Sam! How would I know? Do you look at clocks when you're drunk? And don't tell me you don't get drunk because I've seen you drunker than a skunk!"

"Well, I do put on one now and then, but not on the job. And I don't drive drunk!"

"A bunch of the guys were still around. Bulldozer threw me in that damn hot tub then threw me on one of those cots the drivers use at the other end of the warehouse. He may remember the time. But Irish can tell you — he was the designated driver. How was he killed, anyway? It's hard to believe what George said. A shovel and pruning shears?"

"Whoever did it was damned mad. Kinda reminded me of what the guys from Vietnam used to say about you. That's why I came over."

"You think I killed him?" Jacob looked at the sheriff in disbelief, then shook his head no. "It goes without saying that most anyone would've wanted to, and I'm no different."

"Just implied a question, didn't say that you did. But whoever did it was mad as hell! I've never seen anything like it. I'd have to say he deserved it. Buck — you know the one he gambled with — he came over this morning and told me that Murdock told him last night that he killed those women and threatened to kill Betty's husband."

"Well I'll be damned. He confessed to Buck?"

"I've never known Buck to lie about anything that important."

"How's Mrs. Murdock taking her nephew's death?"

"Doing better than anyone expected. She's making all the arrangements for the funeral. She tried for years to change him, gave him every opportunity but he was just bad, mean and lazy. Buck told me that he had been too scared of Murdock to say anything before, and Mable probably felt the same. Don't think I mind much that

Jack's dead. According to Hiram, he would have walked. There just wasn't enough evidence to convict him. This has saved the taxpayer the price of a trial, but I don't like vigilante justice. It's against the law, but I can understand that kind of anger when I think of those women he killed."

"No matter what the justice, it doesn't fit the crime, or change the horror of what Murdock did, does it Sam?"

"Whoever got Jack came as close to fitting the justice as I've ever seen, but it doesn't bring back those sweet women if that's what you mean. It does clear up several other murders in the past, I'm thinking."

"Sam, I know you're just doing your job. I was on a pity party last night. Upset about my situation, certainly not considering anyone else's. Irish is the tall guy with red hair. He can tell you what time we got back. What time was Murdock killed anyway?"

"Coroner says around one o'clock."

"Alice Ennis was working at the Waffle House. Maybe she can tell you what time we left there. Now tell me, Sam. Are you going to run again? The time is near."

"I'm considering it. Will you back me?"

"I'm thinking about it, but considering my circumstances, do you think I should declare for you? Could do you more harm than good. Who's running against you?"

Sam looked at him and said, "I sure hope to hell it isn't you!" He was grinning like a fool.

"No sweat, Sam. I'm not interested in public office. I'm half owner of this country club."

The Sheriff's cellular phone rang. He pulled it from his pocket and flipped it open. "Sam here!" He listened for a minute then said, "Okay! Nothing here, I'll meet you over at Mable's to see if we missed anything." He hung up the phone and turned to Jacob. "Well, gotta go. Just let me know if you hear anything I should know. Hope you'll be on my team in the fall. I'm headed for Mable's. She makes the best damn pound cake you ever ate — maybe she'll offer me a slice."

"Do I hear wedding bells, Sheriff?"

They both laughed and he answered, "With Murdock around I couldn't go over there. Now, who knows what will happen? I'd sure hate to admit that whoever took care of that bastard did me a favor."

Jacob knew that Sam thought he did it and as long as the attention was focused on him, and he had a good alibi, Dozer would be free to roam. "You can count on my support, Sam. I like your ethics."

Jacob watched the sheriff leave. He knew what the men would say, should Sam ask them anything. He didn't think Sam would look too hard for the killer. He didn't have to because before nightfall everyone in the town of thirty thousand law-abiding citizens knew about Murdock's confession to Buck. The incident would be whisked out the door like yesterday's dirt. Everyone would figure Betty Sue's husband did it, even if he did have an airtight alibi.

Some people have to make the world safe for women and children, Jacob considered. And he knew that Sam felt the same.

Chapter 12

In a room on the fourth floor of the Marriott, two agitated men walked back and forth, never taking their eyes from one another. One was Phil Williams and the other was Nate Smith, a man of unnatural proportions. Nate was over six feet three with bulldog jowls and a heavy Dr. Watson mustache, topped by a balding high-domed head with strands of gray hair growing from one side pulled over to give lie to his baldness. He sported a belly attesting to far too much good food and beer and had the pasty red-white skin of an alcoholic. His normal unctuous manner now transformed to anger.

Phil did not like this man, a contact for hired shooters. "How was your shooter killed? How the hell did that happen?" Phil Williams asked.

"You told us this would be an easy job. What you did not do was warn us that she had a boyfriend, a career Marine! That little evasion got my best man killed! The fucker shot him right between the eyes! I'm telling you, my man was the best there is! And another thing, I won't send any more of my men to that kind of slaughter."

"I gave you all the information I had. It's up to you to gather whatever information you need to do the job. I don't pay for unprofessional fuck-ups!" Phil was sweating; he had not told Nate about the first man: the professional, the man who never failed, who had disappeared without a trace. Belligerently, he asked, "Where's my money?"

Both were tall men and Nate walked right up to Phil and stood nose to nose. "Unprofessional? Your money?"

Nate looked him in the eye. "Call the police. Half of it is in their lockup. I'm sure they'll give it back to you along with a few questions. The rest will bury my man. Just remember it could be arranged to put two in the same box!"

Phil suddenly felt wary. This whole thing was getting out of hand. It should have been so simple. As long as he had known Mary she had always been alone. "All right! I understand that you did try. Keep the fucking money! Just cancel the contract! It's too hot just now with the police investigating. I'll handle it myself."

Nate picked up his raincoat and folded it neatly over his arm. "I can't say it's been a pleasure working with you, but it has been enlightening. However, one word to anyone about me and you will follow my late shooter." He opened the door, then closed it without ever taking his eyes off Phil.

Phil waited a few minutes until he heard the elevator stop, then leave. He yanked off the wig and glasses and put on a crushable hat, pulled a bag from his pocket and put the items inside. Then he pulled off his windbreaker, rolled it into a tight neat ball and added it to the contents of the bag. Pulling down his blue golf shirt, he headed for the elevator. He was dialing as he walked. He heard Martin answer and said, "Meet me around the corner at the bar."

Phil was on his second scotch when Martin Long slid into the booth across from him. "What's up?"

"Your perfect man failed. He's dead. That's the second one! I lost the money and still have the problem."

To Martin the money was no problem. What annoyed him far more was what he would not tell Phil. Someone was on to their game. One assassin killed would be the law of averages; two just couldn't be coincidence.

"According to the paper, there was an exchange of gunfire and the boyfriend got lucky. That was the gist of the report."

"Lucky?" Phil Williams' face screwed up in disbelief.

"That boyfriend put a bullet between the shooter's eyes! That wasn't luck, that was damn straight shooting!"

While Martin Long was trying to calm a distraught Phil Williams, Jacob D.R. Reynolds was sitting in the newly painted first shooter's truck watching Barfus and his wife enter an exclusive restaurant. He waited until all was quiet, then pulled the first assassin's silenced .22 and put a bullet in the radiator of the colonel's new car. The steady downpour would conceal the leak until the car overheated. He shifted gears on the Dodge Ram and drove slowly out of the parking lot.

One thing for sure, Barfus had never walked the jungle. The bastard was going to be a piece of cake. Opening his phone, Jacob dialed a number and waited through four rings before a sexy voice answered with a breathy hello.

"Hello, darling. Are you free tonight?"

"I don't believe the voice I'm hearing. Is this the same man who turned me down because he was loyal to his wife?"

"Things change."

"I heard and I'm sorry. I didn't have anything to do with what they did. I may be low at times, but never that low."

Paydirt! Jacob thought. "How low can you get?"

"For you? Don't confine me. I've seen what you have to offer. However, I fear information is what you have in mind, not my gorgeous body . . . and that will cost you."

"What will it cost me?"

"One night with you."

"I get to choose the place?"

"If you like. I'll meet you halfway."

"Tell you what, leave your apartment now and walk downstairs and straight out the door. You'll see a dark blue Dodge truck with tinted windows and a sexed up bastard sitting behind the wheel."

Marge laughed as she threw on a short skirt and a fur jacket with nothing underneath. She had wanted Reynolds ever since she had met him. If she had to burn Barfus she would, whatever it took. She knew he did not want her, but that didn't matter.

A sudden vision of the colonel and what he would do to her if he found out gave her a chill. Just thinking of what he'd made her do to protect her sister spurred her on, as did the anticipation that a tryst with Jacob would be the same as rubbing Barfus' nose in the mud.

Carrying a lap rug and a bag with jeans and personals, she didn't wait for the elevator but skipped lightly down the steps.

He opened the door just as she emerged from the building and she slid easily in beside him. "Here and now, or later?"

"Give me twenty minutes to get to where we're going, okay? Damn, you're still as beautiful as ever."

"I also have a health card. Clean as a whistle, want to see it?"

"No. I'll take your word. I know you wouldn't lie about something that important."

"Where are we going?"

"I have a place about twenty minutes away."

"I'm not sure I can wait that long." She slid one perfectly manicured nail down the front of his trousers, then replaced it with her finger tips, then her whole hand. "I can see that I won't be disappointed. You're a horny devil tonight. I must've done something right."

Jacob made the twenty minute drive in ten minutes, thinking that if a policeman stopped them she would probably fuck him too. He stopped to open the gate. Carrying a bottle of Scotch, she caught up to him as the gate swung open. She pulled him down in the field of clover beside the driveway, unbuckled his belt and proceeded to play until he was beyond ready. Then she straddled him, took a drink from the bottle and began to ride the horse.

Later, he took a long swig of the Johnny Walker Black, thinking, there's something to be said for a professional. They staggered to the truck and headed for the cabin. He stopped the truck before the door, aware of the busy head in his lap. They staggered to the big shower, and then slick with bath oil they loved their way across the floor, finally winding up in the bed.

It was around ten a.m. the next morning when he awoke. He quietly watched her sleeping. She was curled up with one hand on his shoulder, keeping contact. God! he thought, how childlike she is. She looked so innocent sleeping there, a beautiful child, yet he knew she was twenty-six. He felt a deep compassion, and not just a little bit of guilt, thinking of Annabelle.

Her sleepy, soft big blue eyes opened slowly, then suddenly wide awake, she smiled and said, "Don't you dare touch me! I'm so damned sore I couldn't walk a chalk line. In all my life this is the only time I've ever been totally satisfied. It was worth whatever information you want."

"Marge, little darling, you made me forget that was why I called."

"You sweet liar! If that was the truth, I'd be a virgin."

"Tell me about Bo."

"Jacob, please don't hurt Bo! He's a nothing, a go-fer, and not even a good lawyer, according to Barfus. They use him and his old family contacts, that's all. He told me he didn't do any work on your case. It was all done by Barfus and Ancell Dart and backed by someone named Martin. I only saw him once, and then only a glance because he didn't want me to see him."

"That man, Martin, what did he look like? Was Martin a first or last name?"

"Don't know about the name—that was all I heard. He was kinda short, wiry, one of those men who walk like they own the world. You know, confident stance, expensive suit and he had a black cashmere overcoat draped over his arm. He bullied Bo a bit, arguing with him, so that Bo eventually signed the papers. Bo keeps an apartment downtown and I peeked through the bedroom door to see who it was — that was about six months ago. I heard him call Barfus *fussy.*"

"*Fussy?*"

"It's a nickname some close business associates call Barfus. Bo called me a week ago. Said Barfus had rubbed his face in it that morning about me. I told Bo it was just Barfus' way of trying to get me back. But he said he'd been threatened and he couldn't trust Barfus not to let his wife know in some way. It was then that I realized Barfus had let me have Bo just to have something to hold over Bo's head. Now that he had his leverage he wanted to show me he could control my life. Oh, Jacob! I may not be in love with Bo, but he is gentle, just like a big kid, real clean, good muscles — he works out all the time. Now I'm at the *pig's* beck and call."

Jacob leaned up on one elbow. "The Pig?"

"Barfus. If I don't do what he says, he'll expose my way of life. You see, he found my sister and was going to get her; she was only twelve and my stepfather was going to take money for her — son of a bitch was selling her virginity. I found out and got there first and took her far away. That was ten years ago. She graduated from a private school with honors and is now an RN. She's engaged to be married to a doctor. Barfus is still angry but thinks my step-dad cut him out of the deal for more money. Barfus can ruin me here or anywhere else. I've never been on the street, not even when I was fourteen. I wouldn't know how or what to do."

"Marge, you're some more woman, I'll give you that. Have you ever thought of getting a straight job?"

"I tried that, and the men worried me to death. Every man who hired me wanted the same thing and when I didn't put out, they fired me. One told me plainly that I would not get a job in this town if I wasn't fucking somebody."

Jacob felt a deep anger, the kind his alter ego, D.R.,

felt before a battle, and a calm determination to solve Marge's problem.

"He'll know I was here, Jacob. Maybe he won't know when I left or exactly where I went, but he will know I was with you."

Jacob saw the fear in her eyes even though she was not expressing that fear verbally.

"Marge, I have a friend south of Atlanta who has a huge old house that he's rambling around in all alone — except for some Vietnamese friends who help him keep up the place. Will you let me take you down there for a little while? That place is like a resort. He has a pool, tennis courts, horses and has become pretty-much of a recluse since his wife died a year ago. They didn't have any children and he could sure use some cheering up. Barfus couldn't find you there and you could take time to decide what you want to do with your future. What do you think, will you go? Besides, he's a tall dashing gentleman of the old South, in great shape for his age, younger than I am and he would keep you safe."

"Keep me safe?" Marge could see that Jacob meant what he had just said; it was there in his eyes. "Jacob, that would be a novelty. Will he let me have time to myself? You understand what I mean?"

"Yes, I do understand. Boom is a real gentleman, you'll see. You'll be safe with him. I think you'll like him, Marge. He's a very intelligent man. He was a demolition expert during the war, one hell of a man and a handsome dude. Of course, maybe not so good looking as I am — but a close second." He grinned.

"Your modesty becomes you, Jacob. Okay! I'll go. Now, I'm going to take a shower and get dressed. Don't get near me . . ."

"I never go where I'm not invited."

She laughed and leaned over and kissed him. "Thank you, Jacob, you're a beautiful man."

He watched her walk away. She was truly lovely, with reddish brown hair and smooth, perfect skin, long legs and breasts that fit a hand perfectly. Was he crazy taking her to Boom? What was wrong with him? Yet he knew he needed more mind commitment, someone closer to his reality, someone like Annabelle—and he felt a definite twinge of guilt, while smiling to himself, knowing that last night was one night he would never forget.

Jacob had believed Barfus had set his wife up. He had suspected someone had drugged her, possibly used subliminal messages that confused her, instilling ideas of divorce. Marge had confirmed that scenario. But Marge had said it hadn't been Barfus, but the other man, the one named Martin. Sweet, sweet Margaret didn't even know what they had done to her. He berated himself for allowing the divorce. But she had been adamant and had married a Presbyterian minister only six months after the divorce. According to his daughter, Margaret was happy with her new life. Good for Margaret! He grimaced, realizing that he sure as hell wasn't happy with his. But he would see the culprits were well punished; Margaret would be avenged.

Marge interrupted his angry vengeful thoughts. "Jacob! Here's an extra for you. The Pig has a new friend . . . she's been on the street since she was thirteen. The only thing is, she's only fourteen now, and he knows her age. I had hoped Barfus would leave me alone when he took up with her. Then he pulled this thing with Bo. The girl's name is Maggie Rasher—a little shy sexy redhead. She hates him but she likes the money. She said he tried to get rough with her but she gave it back and he backed down."

Combing her long wavy hair, she looked over one bare, lightly tanned shoulder. "I don't think Bo knows what they're doing—honest to God! That guy was clean, except for me. It was his first affair since his marriage. He felt awfully guilty."

"Don't kid yourself, Marge. Of course he knows. He just tries to keep his nose clean. But don't worry, it isn't Bo that I am after. I won't hurt Bo. I promise you that."

"Thanks, Jacob. Even though I'll never see him again, I don't want to see him hurt. You know, kids and dumb animals . . ."

Much later they were driving up the long lane leading to Boom's house. "My God! Jacob! Is that a house or a hotel?"

"That, my dear, is *Ellenberg Plantation*." Jacob remembered that time and time again in Vietnam, Terry — short for Terrence Mahoney Ellenberg, IV and nicknamed "Boom" by the Marines — had talked about his little country place. He had returned from the war too blunt and outspoken for the gentle folk he had left behind.

They rang the bell and a Vietnamese man answered the door. "Mista Dead Reckon! It is very pleasant to see you again, sir!"

"The pleasure is all mine, Sunny. Where's the old man?"

A deep voice spoke from behind Sunny. "Who is it, Sunny?"

"Boom, it is Mista Dead Reckon and a lovely lady."

"Well, damned if it isn't! You old son of a gun! It's about time you came for a visit. Now who is this lovely lady?"

"Marge, this lanky version of Clark Gable is my old friend, Boom. Boom, this is Marge LeVan."

"Hello, Marge LeVan. Please come in. It's too late for lunch and too early for whiskey, so how about a little tea party in the library? Sunny, will you ask Cookie to make some sandwiches and tea?"

"Yes sir! I'll be only a minute."

Understanding passed between the two old war buddies. They were walking into the library as they talked. A fire burned in the grate of a marble faced fireplace and a big bow window looked out over pastures where horses grazed.

"Boom, this is some more place you have," Marge said.

"Yeah! It's a very rough life," Boom said, smiling.

Sunny brought in a tray with tea and sandwiches and small cakes. "I need to see to that new colt. Just ring me at the stable if you need me. Happy to see you again, D.R.!"

"The pleasure is all mine, Sunny! Give Cookie a hug for me on your way out."

"Okay D.R.! I can tell by the expression on your face that something is up and I've heard some rumors from the guys, so what do you want me to do?"

"What I need is simple enough, Boom. A man I don't like has his claws out for Marge and I'm looking for a place of safety for her. I thought of you rambling around in this big old house all alone. I know he'd never find her here. I could get lost in all these rooms. What would you say about having a beautiful guest for a couple of months?"

Marge looked down at her lap, then lifted her eyes to look at Terrance (Boom) Mahoney Ellenberg from under her long lashes. "I'm afraid I had to leave with only the clothes I'm wearing." The forlorn look in her eyes would have melted iron.

"Don't worry, lovely lady, I happen to know of several establishments that can remedy the situation. Do I detect a hint of exhaustion behind those pretty eyes?"

Marge looked at Jacob, then at Boom. "I am a little tired."

Boom picked up a phone. "May, please come to the library. We have a guest, a lady, and I need you to show her to the pink guestroom. Also, get a robe and gown from the upstairs closet and anything else you can find that might fit. Her luggage was lost by the airline." He turned to Marge. "May will be here in a minute. She'll take you upstairs. Please make yourself at home; rest as long as you like. Dinner is at seven-thirty and I hope you will join me. I'm very pleased to have you as my guest and I hope you'll be comfortable here with us. Just ask May for anything you need and if it isn't here, she'll put it on a list to get when she goes into town."

"You're very generous, sir."

May came in smiling and was introduced — an older woman, gray hair cut to shape her head, she was almost as round as she was tall with a dimpled smile and a crisp efficient manner. Marge gave Jacob a kiss and a quiet thank you, then followed May out and up the main staircase. Both men walked with her to the stairs and stood mesmerized as Marge gave them her best walk up the wide staircase.

"D.R., you must be losing it. You actually trust me with her? Just watching her walk up those stairs makes my balls jump and say howdy!"

"Actually, Boom, you may not be safe with her — but the finding out will probably be just what you need. She's some more woman . . . if I didn't have Annabelle . . . whew! Marge has information I will eventually need to get myself reinstated. When Barfus finds his protégé gone, he'll beat the countryside searching. She knows he's having an affair with an underage girl, not to mention what she has learned these past ten years."

"Old Barfus is still around? He was a sorry ass when I knew him years ago. I'll keep Marge safe, you can count on it!"

"Boom, do you mind if I rush off? I'll keep in touch as often as I can without giving away her location."

"D.R.?"

"Yeah?"

"Let me in on the trouble. The intensity I see behind your eyes reminds me of a feeling I sometimes get when I start to defuse a charge. Somebody is in for trouble . . . deep trouble."

"Maybe. Keep a light in the window."

"You'll call me if you need me?"

"I just did. Keep her safe for us all, Boom."

"My pleasure."

"Could be, if you bank your charges right!"

Chapter 13

Jacob Reynolds picked up his pace crossing the field. Damn! He would never get used to that awful smell. The daily drum burning of oil and excrement had begun and the nasal revulsion was intense. He knew that odor would stay with him forever, tucked away in a fold of his sensory cells, no matter how he tried to purge the stench.

He had left the aircraft line and was headed straight for supply, making a mental list of what he would need — including a body bag if he didn't get back in time to save the boy. There was no question of not going. Marines did not leave their own behind.

He had just finished refueling when Boom walked up. "What do you think you're doing?"

"Going back for a boy in Laos."

"The one Anderson left behind?"

"Word travels fast."

"Yeah. He wasn't supposed to have that signal. He lost Willis and left Miller carrying him. He disobeyed orders. He's in a heap of trouble."

"Not in my book. He had no other choice. He had to try to get his men out. They were in a wedge with NVA on three sides and a sheer cliff on the other. Either they got lost or were misinformed. If you'd been there and seen how many NVA's there were, you would understand. We're lucky any got out alive. Besides, Willis didn't die in vain. By being at that particular spot they blew the NVA's surprise attack."

"You volunteered to go back?"

"I have to go back, Boom. I saw the kid's eyes. I can't pilot and be on the ground at the same time. Gotta see who's available. We aren't supposed to be there so we need someone who can drop us as close as possible. Then when we get Miller and Willis, they can extract us. Mostly it's grunt work, but still, some volunteers would be welcome . . ."

"Just hold up. I'll be back in a few minutes."

Boom returned soon with a tall, skinny guy he called 'Irish'. A black bandanna covered Irishs' red hair, except for the tip of a pigtail. He was armed for quick fighting at close range, carrying a well-cleaned short stock automatic in a waterproof sling over the shoulder of his utilities. The dull black handle of another gun protruded from a pocket on his right leg. On his left thigh were two sheaths holding narrow-handled throwing knives. That was all that was visible.

Behind 'Irish' stood a huge brute of a man known simply as 'Bulldozer'. At first glance, he looked fat, but it was only the loose utilities that he wore. Huge biceps and pec's sculpted the material of his shirt as he moved, revealing a quick, muscular body. He had a broad face with a cleft chin that jutted out even with his nose. A permanent frown creased his forehead. On his head was a circle of leaves with tiny branches sticking out. He would definitely be Victor Charlie's May Day nightmare.

Boom had been an amazement to D.R. since they had met on his first tour. He was a tall, slim and elegant southern gentleman who wore his uniform as if it were a tuxedo. New recruits had often made the mistake of thinking his gentle manners made him a sissy, when in reality he was a very *sudden* black-belted gentleman.

Boom bowed. "It is a pleasure to travel with you gentlemen. D.R., may I present Mr. Chew Marron, our pilot. Chew is from Oklahoma where in order to get a pilots license one must pick squirrels off power lines by hand."

D.R. was looking at a tall, gangly man with blonde hair that stuck out like Dagwood and a nose that would best Groucho Marx. A substantial bulge in his jaw revealed the source of his nickname, but it was the man's eyes that caught D.R.'s attention; they were the most humorous he had ever seen. If there were secrets in the world, Chew Marron knew them all and found them amusing. Chew left them to check out the aircraft.

D.R. watched Chew as he climbed up into the helo and melted his big lanky body down into the pilot's seat; then his long fingers began flipping switches as smoothly as a pianist playing a familiar lullaby. Watching the long-limbed smiling man make the chopper his own, D.R. knew that if anyone would get them in and out this man could.

Chew dropped them within sight of their goal, but it would take at least two hours to get there over the rough terrain. Once on the trail, Irish, the West Virginia mountain man, took point. He had an instinct for this war zone that had kept him alive for over two years.

They didn't talk, just listened.

Every so often Bulldozer, pulling rear guard, would disappear, find a spot and wait. He was well hidden, a relaxed part of the land, when six Charlie's came through. Somehow they had picked up a sign or had spotted the aircraft and were spread out searching for signs. He fell in behind them silently, taking them out one by one.

Irish stopped in the shade of a stream and in sign language indicated a rest stop to wait for Dozer. Twenty minutes later, Bulldozer appeared. They watched as he washed his hands and arms in the swiftly running water. He pulled out a mega-muscle bar and squatted beside the stream. In sign language, he told them, "Six VC's cut your trail and were about to fuck your ass." He conveyed the message in several very simple signs.

D.R. was on his third tour in Vietnam. He was damned good and he knew it, but he was not up to these two. Irish was almost running at point without hitting a trap. D.R. felt like dead weight in comparison.

Boom didn't seem surprised, just nodded to his friend. D.R. would have liked to get the story on Bulldozer and

Irish from Boom, but they couldn't talk while in the jungle.

Two hours later they reached the bottom of the rock precipice where he had last seen the young Marine. They found Willis tucked snugly between some upright boulders at the bottom of the cliff. Miller had done well; the body had not been mutilated.

Bypassing the well-marked trail, carrying Willis, they made their own way to the top. Keeping to the shadows, they reconned the area for the other Marine. Irish's expertise was nosing out booby traps, and Boom, the explosive expert, dismantled them.

It didn't take the hair standing up on the back of his head to warn D.R. that the North Vietnamese Regular Army battalion had left some men behind. He wiggled through the underbrush and saw two NVA's sitting relaxed, cooking rice on a small fire in a circle of rocks. There was another keeping watch to D.R.'s right. He motioned Irish to circle to his left. Only then did he notice the silencer on the gun Irish had drawn.

It was Jacob's alter ego, Dead Reckon, or D.R. as they called him, who silently crept up on the NVA sentry and made sure he never killed another Marine. Then he crawled closer to the two men cooking rice. The men suddenly looked up, eyebrows raised as though looking for a friend, and then a small hole appeared just above the bridge of their noses. Who had they expected? It certainly wasn't death, for they had not been alarmed. Fear for Irish seared his brain. He was sure they had been expecting their own men. Irish had squatted beside the fire and was eating hot rice from the pot.

D.R. moved quickly from one shadow to another, watching for any movement. Then he saw them — three NVA's coming single file down a trail that led directly beneath him. They were talking quietly, heading for where Irish sat eating their lunch.

D.R. had learned a lot of Vietnamese in the past two tours. They were still looking for the other Marine; they wanted to parade him through North Vietnam. He threw a pebble to warn Irish, then dropped to the trail behind what he hoped was the last NVA. He got one, the others walked on, and then one turned to look back, saw it wasn't his companion but his worst nightmare behind him, and his surprise became eternal.

The other turned on D.R. but didn't get a chance to use his gun. Stepping aside, D.R. let Irish finish the job. There had been no noise to warn any other NVA's in the area of their presence. Stealthily, they returned to where Boom and Bulldozer were disarming the booby traps.

"I heard what they were saying. They haven't found the Marine. I'll bet he's still where I last saw him. No way he could have gotten out with all those gooks around."

Bulldozer signaled that there were more. Irish held up six fingers and then turned them down and held up one. He had found recent footprints of seven men.

D.R. crawled to the edge of the ridge where he had last seen Miller, but there was no way down. The ledge Miller had used to climb down was now at the bottom of the cliff; it must have given way with the weight of both men. There was an overhanging root mass the Marine might have used to keep from falling.

"Bulldozer! Hold my feet and let me down slow . . . I don't want him to take my head off." Pulling himself over the ledge he eased his way down the cliff. He spoke softly, "Lee Miller! Where are you, man?" He heard a movement. Again he called, "Miller! It's Reynolds. We're here to get you out."

Scraping sounds, then a hand came over the edge, and then the top of a sweaty blond head. The boy was cautious. His gun came up and he rolled face up. "Dammit, Skipper, where the hell have you been? I've been waiting on this fucking rock all my life with NVA pissing all around me."

"Give me your hand and we'll pull you out." D.R. had Miller half over the top of the cliff when he felt the sting in his back before he heard the rifle's report. The muscles in his right arm went slack, and then he began to feel the pain. Miller had a firm hold on his right arm and wasn't about to let go. Bulldozer, seeing the impact and D.R. faltering, yanked D.R. and Miller back from the edge, rolling backward with both men, behind a boulder.

Irish took the sniper out before he could do any more damage, but D.R. was bleeding profusely from a nasty wound in his back just below his right shoulder blade.

Boom dressed the wound, momentarily stopping the flow of blood with the pressure of his hand over the bandage. He then called Chew to pick them up. Boom had been right about Chew, he plucked them off the ridge right where they were standing; then they got the hell out of Laos.

That bullet took D.R. off flight status and he finished his tour as a pentagon *gofer*. It didn't take him long to figure out why the war was a bust: McNamara, Ford's boy genius.

Jacob D.R. Reynolds shook his head to erase the memory. He was in his Land Rover on the freeway headed back to Atlanta, but the memory was as vivid as that day on the mountain in Laos. He had not heard from Miller since; he hoped the boy had made it through his enlistment.

He off-ramped to a Quick Stop for some coffee to try to stop the shaking inside, amazed that it still happened even after all those years. Most of the time he could control those emotions, but other times the angry frustration at the loss of so many good men was just too much for him to absorb. He wondered how war could be held up to be so exciting when it was the most horror a soul could encounter. Being well trained didn't make it any easier. It only meant he was better than some at the job and more likely to stay alive while doing that job — something one big law firm was about to find out.

Chapter 14

A puzzled frown squinted Jacob's bright green eyes as three sheriff's cars with lights flashing came roaring in from three directions. One came across the empty lot to the left, leaving curls of dust clouds in its wake. Jacob had been watching Bulldozer's men loading three new gleaming yellow machines on their heavy wood and metal trailers. Soon they would be on the job earning their keep.

A vision of the colonel's yacht slowly sinking flashed across his mind. He could have put him away right then but when he did, he wanted to be face to face—wanted him to know who and what he had breached. He smiled, remembering the panic on old Barfus' face as he scurried around, carrying his clothes in one hand, trying to get the naked young man off the boat before anyone saw him. That Barfus was a sexual switch hitter was just another degenerate trait. D.R. had felt sad for Elizabeth Barfus. The pictures should turn out perfectly. He quickly went over every action the night before, and could spot no screw up, so he was surprised at this unusual hustle by the police.

Two men jumped from cars on either side of Sam's and threw the menacing barrels of shotguns over the top of the open doors. Jacob heard the men scrambling behind him and knew they were going for weapons. Bulldozer ran up beside him. "Hold the men back, Dozer. We don't want any trouble with Sam." Dozer flicked his wrist to the men waiting in the warehouse. Jacob stood still waiting for Sam to get out and explain what was happening.

All he needed was for one of those greenhorns to get

an itchy finger. Sam's boys didn't know what a curly tiger was and he sure hoped they didn't try to take one by the tail. It wasn't that he was afraid to die. God knew he had earned it. He didn't want the deputies to die, though, for die they would if they squeezed a trigger.

"Damn it, Sam! This looks like a raiding party," Jacob said.

Sam walked toward the police cars and yelled at his men, "Put those goddamn weapons away! You want to get yourselves killed. Get in those cars and leave. Now! Who the hell called you out here?"

One of the men put down his gun and walked sheepishly around the car door. "The DA told us to meet him here because he expected trouble."

"The DA should have told me, not you."

Sam stopped at the bottom of the steps. "Jacob, I've got bad news. You have to come downtown with me."

"Okay, Sam, whatever you say. What's the problem?" Jacob spoke while walking down the steps, hands in the open. Then he walked up to Sam, stopped and turned around. "There's a gun in a holster in the back of my slacks; I have a permit, but I will not touch the gun. You get it, Sam." He grinned at Bulldozer. They both knew it would be no contest should they make that decision.

"I won't cuff you, Jacob, but this is serious. Get in front beside me."

Before that could happen, another car drove up. "The fucking leech," Sam said, glaring at the approaching vehicle. "He had to be in on the arrest, hoping to make the headlines. Look, Jacob, he even brought a reporter and photographer. This is a set up if I ever saw one."

Jacob turned to his friend. "Wait a minute, Sam, let's see what he has to say."

"Well, well the great ex-counselor Jacob Reynolds. We've got you this time!" The DA was all smiles, holding a warrant like he was about to swat a fly, a knowing satisfaction giving him whiskey courage. But the hard, cold look in D.R.'s sudden death green eyes gave him pause. He stopped and stepped back.

His presence was usually enough to intimidate most men, yet this man facing arrest wasn't scared. For the first time, he really looked at Reynolds, and suddenly he felt a fear like none he had ever experienced, a feeling that he, not Jacob, was a rabbit caught in a snare. His knees suddenly felt weak and he wanted to turn and run. The man was formidable; those knowing eyes cut to his very core, exposing weaknesses he had long refused to acknowledge. But Jacob Reynolds knew he could take him. He shuddered with a quick intake of breath, then remembered he had the law on his side.

Jacob saw the DA's fear exposed in his pale blue eyes and the satisfaction was his. He reached out and took the warrant, read it, then spoke to the men on the dock. "He has a warrant to search my office. See that's all he does."

Bulldozer and Irish walked to the steps leading to Jacob's office. The DA hesitated, aware he would have to walk in close proximity to the men who looked as tough as Jacob. Reynolds was an honorable man; he wouldn't let Sam down, so the DA and his assistant walked up the steps, keeping a wary eye on the big man standing so close. They could smell the mingling of sweat and aftershave when they slipped by him so close they touched muscles hard as stone. The DA avoided looking in the big man's eyes, but his assistant was not so knowledgeable.

Tim Morrison looked up into the most deadly eyes he had ever seen and stopped like a rabbit frozen in the eyes of a lion. Bulldozer smiled and said, "Move on little boy, you're not a fly on my swatter yet. See that you don't become one."

The DA turned back and said, "Are you threatening my assistant?"

"I don't rightly know. Was I threatening you, boy?"

Instinctively, Tim knew that no district attorney could protect him from this man, and in that instant he became wise. "No! Of course not." Tim's feet found the next step; he could not believe his whimpering insides. He dropped his eyes and followed his boss into Jacob's office. He was young and had never met a real mean SOB before. Never again would he respect the DA. If Reynolds was the same sort, my God! What were they doing? Holding out his small hands, he felt totally inadequate as a man, although he was twenty-eight years old.

The DA went straight to Jacob's office. That's interesting, Bulldozer thought. How did he know which office was Jacob's? There were now three offices in that part of the building. A plant among his own men? "Stay with him Irish," he said, hurrying to the door. "Hold up just a minute, Sam."

"Jacob, has the DA ever been over here before?"

"Not to my knowledge."

"Then how did he know which office was yours?"

"Good question. I know you'll look into it. Just find the sneak. Don't do anything that Sam would have to investigate, right Sam?" Jacob knew Bulldozer wouldn't go against Sam, but the DA was another matter altogether. "Dozer, call Swaney, have him meet me at the jail." Dozer just nodded, opening and closing his big fists as he watched Sam drive D.R. away in the squad car.

"Okay! Sam. What's this all about."

"You know that kid you called the ambulance for yesterday afternoon . . . the one that was brutally beaten?"

"Yeah."

Sam bowed his head, then looked off in the distance. "Jacob, that girl had been brutally raped . . . and she named you the rapist."

Jacob took a deep breath. He had wondered what their next move would be. "Sam, did the hospital do a semen check?"

"Yes, but no luck. She was beat about the head, face and breasts. She was hysterical. Gave your description this morning and ID'd your photograph."

"What's the background on the girl?"

"She's visiting her aunt here. That's the puzzle. She's clean as a whistle, no arrests. No sexual activity before the rape, according to the doctor."

"Sam, you can believe that cherry is not on my tree! No way would I ever seduce a young girl, let alone rape one. You know me better than that."

"What I know doesn't count. The DA will prosecute; you know how he works. He will prosecute to the fullest extent of the law. It's all going too smooth, too fast. Looks like everything was arranged before the rape occurred."

"What's the DA's connection to Barfus?"

Sam looked thoughtful. "You think there's a connection between them, you and the rape?"

"No other reason is there? Why would the girl pick me out to accuse if not pointed in my direction by someone with an awful grudge? Why had she even been in the neighborhood of the warehouse? I don't even know why Barfus is after me. It has to be someone else behind him, Sam. Someone I should have killed in the past and didn't."

"You know I hear things, but you probably know more about that law firm than I do. I have heard some gossip over the past year. It's rumored that Barfus likes young stuff, but so far he's kept it clean."

Jacob spoke knowingly, "Until now."

"You think he did it?"

"Had to be, I sure as hell didn't." Then a thought came to him. "Who is her aunt?"

"Mamie Hull, do you know her?"

"Never heard of her. Is she a local?"

"Been here ten years or so, works as a secretary at the school. She keeps pretty much to herself but is well liked. She's been seeing old man Tatum on occasion, but we both know he's too tight to ever marry anyone. I don't know anything about her that we can use."

"Right now I can't even sympathize with that little liar. Why did she do it? For money? Did she know what she was getting into? Had she expected just to get her hymen busted, not knowing the sicko she was dealing with? Sam, she had to have trusted someone and was double-crossed. Whoever, he got his money's worth from her in pain. Who else could it have been but Barfus, with his penchant for young stuff and his determination to destroy me?"

"We have no proof of that. It's just rumor. I agree there's some deep political shit and a lot of money behind whoever is after you."

"Sam, I appreciate your moral support and anything you can find out. Wonder if they'll let me make bail?"

"Don't know. The DA has five fingers on each hand and each finger is tied to an office in the justice system."

"Mind if I make a call on my own phone?"

"Wait, I'm going to stop here and get us a cup of coffee. You can use that payphone just inside the door. Can't take a chance with the cellular. Want a sandwich? They make one hell of good chicken salad."

"Sure, might as well. I don't know how long this will take or when I will eat again."

"I'll get a table. Come on in when you finish."

D.R. dropped a quarter and a dime in the phone and punched in Annabelle's number. She answered right away. "Hello, friend. I need some help. Sam just picked me up. A young girl is yelling rape and says it was me."

"She should be so lucky!"

"No jokes now, this is serious. The DA's running fast. They aren't even waiting for this to go through regular channels."

"What do you want me to do?"

"Just keep your ear to the ground and let me know if you find out anything I can use."

"I'll do more than that, as you well know. I'll talk with you soon. Stay calm, don't do anything foolish."

"You know me better than that."

"They don't know what you're capable of . . . and I do."

"I'll be in touch. Damn! I'm going to miss those orchids. This sure ruins my lovely nights."

"Yeah! Mine too!"

Harold Swaney finished his summation to the jury, then watched as they left to deliberate Jacob Reynolds' fate. Annabelle was waiting with Jacob, so Swaney quickly walked the short distance across the square to his office. His associates, Norm Foxwater and Larry Travis, were waiting with a bottle of his favorite scotch. Seeing how upset Swaney was, Larry quickly poured him five fingers of Johnny Walker Black.

"Summation go as we rehearsed, or did you wing it?" Larry asked.

"I barely deviated from the script. Four of the jurors would not look me in the eyes, so I yelled, 'This is foul! This man is innocent!' That got their immediate attention so I continued, explaining how the prosecution had failed to prove its case. 'All they have produced is circumstantial evidence,' I said. 'They have shown you a coat that a good Samaritan, on finding an injured person beside his company's gate, took off and covered that injured person, then called 911. They have shown you bloody clothing left in a wastebasket in the office of the accused. Believe me, no man to whom minute detail could mean the difference between life and death would ever be that careless . . . Jacob Reynolds is an innocent man! You have heard witnesses to his good character, you have heard the oath he took as a Marine to protect those who cannot protect themselves! This man has been framed! Framed by persons unknown, and the prosecution has failed in its duty by not searching for the *true* perpetrator!'"

Swaney became passionate again as he continued to repeat his summation. "This travesty of justice stinks so highly of frame-up as to be childish in its conception and application. Jacob Reynolds has an air-tight alibi for the time the prosecution says he was abusing this girl. Yet, she still persists in naming him as her attacker! Dr. Ravelar, the examining psychiatrist has told you that the girl is confused and that she does not always tell the truth about what happened to her."

"You, the jury, must see there is a huge crater of

reasonable doubt in this case! There are just too many inconsistencies. You have the opportunity now to reverse this travesty. An opportunity to set an innocent man free! As jurors, all you must do is find reasonable doubt, and there is reasonable doubt beyond belief! You MUST set this innocent man free!"

"Well done, Harold. Very well done. I couldn't have done it any better," Norm said when Swaney had finished. "It was very powerful. If they can't see the truth now, then they're stupid!"

"Thanks, Norm. Let's hope they're not stupid."

Swaney had finished his drink and was contemplating having another when the telephone rang, startling everyone. It was too soon! When a jury comes back that soon the verdict is almost always *guilty*. That thought raced through their minds as Swaney picked up the telephone.

"Good God! The jury is back already!" Swaney yelled. Grabbing his jacket, he rushed across the square and stood beside Jacob as the jury filed in.

The baliff took the piece of paper from the jury spokesperson and handed it to the judge. The judge silently read the verdict, then handed it back to the baliff. He gave it back to the spokesperson, who, upon direction from the judge, read it aloud: "We find the defendent guilty!"

Jacob was in shock. It seemed impossible, but the idiots had found him guilty! More money must have changed hands, he concluded, noting that none of the jury members would look his way. Beside him, Swaney was cursing a blue streak under his breath. He turned to Jacob, "We WILL appeal!"

Prison turned out to be a new experience for Jacob Reynolds, although the animosity he encountered there was not. Even his reputation, which had preceded him, did little to deter those who thought themselves tough. It took his putting five men in the hospital before they finally understood.

Instead of punishment, the warden found a room behind the library and had a desk and bed put in it. "Jacob, just between us, your time is your own so long as the outside doesn't question." From then on Jacob was the 'in residence' counselor helping other inmates with their appeals. Jacob wondered about his status, but didn't question the isolation, which gave him time to study.

He enrolled in a college course studying philosophy, and two years passed faster than he thought. One rainy day in August, as he sat at the desk in his cell, he stopped reading the Koran, which he was studying at the time, and began to think about his soul. He had done a lot of things in his life of which he was not proud. He had been trying to reconcile his past actions with the confusion put forth as religion, knowing if and when he got out that he would go after the men who had put him there. That was a given.

He certainly understood the fundamentals of religion, and understood it was obviously planned to civilize mankind. Most people spouted it but few lived it. Most used it to better themselves, which was good, but not if they used it to preen before their neighbors. It calmed their fears, helped them to forgive themselves or in some cases brought about political gain. Religion helped to maintain a pendulum of morality. Without it, given the chance, most men would revert to primal instincts. He still didn't have a handle on what he really believed, but he was trying to learn by reading the precepts of all the major religions.

One of Boom's friends, Bennie Lane, a skip tracer, had taken it on himself to locate Mamie Hull and her niece who had left town after the trial. He had broken into the bank's computer and found that they had over three hundred thousand dollars in various banks and investment funds. He had traced the deposits and they were all cash. But he was still looking for that amount being withdrawn from other accounts.

One day the phone rang. It was the warden. "The Assistant District Attorney, Grady Beal, will be here soon. I'm going to put your release on the table. I don't want to give you false hope. He is the DA's man all the way, but I'll try to put our little plan to him and see what he says."

"Thanks warden, but I give it little hope."

"There's something I want you to know. I'm sending a guard for you."

The guard, who was a small man of about fifty-three , courteously escorted Jacob to the warden's office, then left. Warden Anderson came forward, hand outstretched. "D.R., you still don't remember me, but you saved my bacon on a mountain in Laos. Since it could be interpreted as special favors, I waited until now to remind you of who I am. Maybe you will remember a platoon surrounded by NVA on a ridge in Laos. You went back for the one left behind. You were wounded and I never got a chance to thank you properly."

"Sorry, I didn't make the connection, Warden. You've changed, as have we all, and I was too busy at the time to even get a good look at you. I remember that you were surrounded with no way out. I'm just glad we were in close proximity and able to get to you in time."

"We'll talk later. The *Ass D* is coming in the gate now. The trustee I'm sending you back with has a message for you. Just go along with him. There's something you need to hear."

"Whatever you want, Warden."

"This way, Skipper." Jacob looked at the trustee again. The man was a veteran. Should he know this man? No bells rang in his mind, so he followed the man to a closet near the library.

"This is the recon room, Sir! Please sit on that overturned bucket and put on these earphones. He untangled another pair and put them on his own ears; then reached behind him and slid a bolt locking the door. In the silence of the closet, he listened to Beal and the Warden.

When it was evident that Beal wasn't in favor of parole for Jacob, the trustee put his earphones down, picked up a ladder and a broom and went out, closing the door behind him.

Jacob opened the door and walked back to the library. The guard at the door looked at him and said, "You don't have an escort?"

"Why would I need one? I'm not going anywhere."

The guard grinned. "That's for sure. Rumor has it that you'll be in here long as there are strings."

"Tell you what, Brad, don't go invest in any string. The law has a way of righting its own wrongs."

Somehow, when the door closed behind him, he felt a sense of relief.

Chapter 15

Smooth mounds of sculpted biceps and pecs strained the starched fabric of the gray blue shirt of the young guard standing at attention just outside the warden's office. A .44 Magnum fit easily in a holster on a belt custom made for his weightlifter waist. With a countenance of affable courtesy, he spoke to the man who had just walked angrily out of Warden Anderson's office. "Please watch your step, sir."

The man turned his haughty intimidating expression on the guard. A shammy skin-covered stick slid as silently as a snake through the ornate grillwork beside the steps, coming to rest on the step just below the foot that was poised to descend.

Grady Beal made a quick assessment of the guard and thought he was being condescending. His conceit tempted him to lightly skip down to the next step, lifting the back foot before the front one was well settled. The trip stick did its work. Beal suddenly realized he was falling and his expression turned to one of horror as he realized he could not stop. He grabbed for the railing, but his forward momentum pulled his hand just out of reach. The guard yelled and tried to catch him, but too late, as he watched in horrified fascination while the man fell headfirst to the concrete landing below. He ran down the steps shouting into his radio for the prison doctor. It was only a couple of minutes before Doc Patterson hurried to the man's side.

The yelling brought Warden Anderson from his office. He stood on the landing looking down the steps. "My God!

Is that the Assistant District Attorney, Grady Beal?" He hurried down the steps.

Doc Patterson looked up. "Yes! He hit on his head; I can't bring him around. It appears that his neck is broken." He turned to the guard. "Harry! Get an ambulance here ASAP!"

A few minutes later, Warden Anderson, Doctor Patterson and Harry Malone stood watching the ambulance disappear in the distance. "Well Doc, what do you think? Will he live? And if so, will he blame me for his fall?"

"Don't know how he could blame you, Sir." It was Harry who answered Anderson's question. "I warned him to watch his step. He looked back at me, skipped down to the next step, lost his footing and fell. It was just that simple."

"It may not be so simple when the lawyers get hold of it, Harry. I'm aware of your connection to the DA. He may try to force you to tell his version of what happened. You're an honest man, I know that and I know you want to do what is right, without the colonel putting pressure on you. We both know how attorneys can twist the truth and that would not go well with your Christian faith. Just to keep everything honest, why don't you go fax a statement to the press and then to the DA's office in clear and concise English stating just exactly what happened. That way they can't mess with your mind, and your conscience will be in the clear. What do you think?"

"Warden, you're a more understanding man than I've been led to believe. Thank you. For the record, all I did was tell them you let Reynolds use the library."

"Don't worry about it, Harry. We're all just getting through this world the best we can, but honesty is always the best policy. I'll keep your secret, and you can talk with me about anything, anytime. It'll be best if you send that fax before the DA has time to force another story down your throat."

"Yes, you're right. I'll do it now. He won't like it but it will be too late to change the truth."

Anderson didn't even turn to watch him leave. It wasn't necessary, for he could easily hear Harry's quick steps clicking across the stone floor to the office. He knew Harry would think twice before sending any more information to the DA.

Dr. Patterson walked across the short distance to where the warden was standing. The ambulance was now a dot in the distance. "Not much hope for him, I'm afraid. Broken neck and severe concussion. If he does live, he'll be paralyzed from the neck down. May be best if he doesn't make it. It doesn't matter; he probably won't remember your discussion. I gather he didn't comply?"

"No! Just the opposite. He told me I had better look for another job."

"Reynolds do the job on Beal?"

"No! By God! It really was an accident. Can you believe it? Harry was looking right at the man when he fell. Maybe there is a God after all, Pat. I'd better get Jacob Reynolds up here and tell him what happened."

A trustee busily mopping the landing stepped aside to let them pass.

"Where were you when the DA fell?" the warden asked.

"I came around the corner just after he fell. Didn't see what happened. Only saw him on the landing."

"What's your name?"

"James Lee Miller, sir!" As he spoke, he removed a polishing cloth from his back pocket and began to shine the grillwork on the steps.

"You're in for drunken assault?"

"Yes sir! The idiot tried to paw my wife. Nobody bothers my wife!"

"You look familiar. Were you in Nam?"

"Not so I can remember, sir!"

"You're doing a good job. Keep your nose clean and you'll be out of here soon."

Walking up the steps, Anderson reviewed his conversation with Grady Beal. He had been pacing the distance before the front windows when the Assistant DA arrived. They had been discussing the early release of Ford James, a drunk driver who had killed a woman in an accident, when he had brought up the possibility of parole for Jacob Reynolds.

He remembered the surprised look on Beal's face as his mind digested what he had just heard. Beal couldn't believe the warden expected him to help get a fifty-five year old felon out of prison, a felon that his boss, the DA, had spent a lot of effort to put there and that some very important people were paying heavily to keep there.

Grady had decided to give Anderson enough rope with which to hang himself. "Okay! So we get this felon paroled, then what? He's been in for two years on circumstantial evidence. If he had been convicted of murder, instead of violent rape, which he wasn't, he would have been out in seven max. We both know he's guilty as hell! It couldn't have been anyone else. The DA thinks he was behind his own accident."

"You people don't have a shred of evidence linking Reynolds to the DA's accident. He could sue you for that accusation. You also know as well as I do that he didn't rape that girl!"

"Nobody else could have done that and you know it, Warden! Now you want me to stick my neck out for this guy? The DA will eat me alive for this kind of treachery. You're crazy! I won't do it!"

"So, you're familiar with Armond Barfus & Associates vs. Jacob Denton Reynolds — oh, I mean the State?"

Grady simply nodded.

Anderson took a deep breath and played his trump card. "A group of people have it on good authority that the DA is on the take."

Grady's mouth dropped open, the accusation ringing in his ears. His fat rump came off the desk. Although he had not been Assistant District Attorney at that time, that trial rang one hell of a bell. "I sure hope you know what you're saying. Accusing the DA of anything is serious business, and I have a family to support."

Warden Anderson looked Beal directly in the eyes to watch his reaction to his next comment. "We have a witness to the transaction. There is absolutely no doubt."

"I don't suppose you would tell me the name of your witness?"

"Last Thursday you picked up an envelope at Armond Barfus and Associates on Magnolia Boulevard." Beal's red face suddenly turned even redder. "You left there and met the DA for lunch at Brevard's Restaurant. During the course of the meal the DA asked for the envelope. He was so anxious to know if it was all there that he opened the envelope in his secluded corner of the restaurant to take a peek. We have it all on video."

Sweat formed tiny globs that began to descend Grady's forehead, following the frown lines that had suddenly appeared. He walked to the window and looked out. He rubbed his broad hands with stubby fingers through his wavy red hair. "You know that won't wash in a courtroom. We'll tear it apart. How do you know that wasn't drug money taken in a raid that had been turned over to me and that I was giving to the DA for safe keeping? If that's all you have, you don't have shit!"

"I have you . . ." It was cold fact spoken in tones of steel.

"If this is a form of prison blackmail, I don't scare easily."

"Beal, you head the investigation. You put him away, or we do it and you go down with him."

"Some choice . . ." He was embarrassed, horrified actually, that his own dirty laundry had been so skillfully thrown in his face. The details were too specific. He knew exactly how much the DA had taken over the past four years and how much of that had landed in his own pocket. They probably already knew he paid cash for everything.

"In or out, Grady?"

"What happens afterward?"

"You resign, find a nice quiet job in some out of the

way place and we never hear from you again."

They both knew that might not be possible; the trial could bring out yet another trial, Grady's own. He also knew it was a chance Grady had to take.

Grady was mulling the possibilities, wondering who else might be in this with the warden? *Accidents happen*, he thought, *even in a prison.*

"Grady, we've only known each other for about four years. I'm fully aware that you're here because the DA brought you here. If you aren't inclined to help me, you sure as hell better not hurt me on this. There's no need to remind you that a lot of good men owe their freedom to Jacob Denton Reynolds."

"Okay! Saying I go along with you, who else will I be working with?"

Listening with the earphones, Jacob heard the deceit in Grady's voice. Grady was trying to find a hole to wiggle through and if that hole meant killing the lot of them, he would find a way. From now on the warden's life would be in danger.

"I will be your only contact. You will not know or meet the others. By the way, Grady, this isn't anything personal, the DA is just way out of hand. You know about Martin Gold, David Lean, Michael Martin — all innocent men who took the fall for Barfus' nephew, Jimmy Hall, on that other rape case. Why else did Barfus go to so much expense to get them paroled? Not to mention sending his nephew to Australia on an extended visit. Can you imagine what this will do to the public trust?"

Grady turned from the window. "My God, how high have you people gone? Do you realize what you're doing? Armond Barfus will eat you alive in court. You won't stand a fucking chance! You know damn fucking well that I will be impaled the first time I testify. Even if we pretend it is MY investigation."

"In or out, Grady?"

"I need to think about this?"

"What you mean is you need to discuss this with the

DA. Either you're in or you're out, right now!" The finality of the decision was clear in his voice.

"Sink with Dan Hollis or swim with you sharks?" He stood up, picked a piece of lint off his left sleeve. "If you need me, you don't have a case. No deal!"

Anderson wanted to strangle the bastard. Jacob had agreed to give Grady a chance. They had hoped to save the Beal children their father's disgrace. He sighed. "Have it your way, Grady. Just remember, I offered you a liferaft and you refused."

"I'm not so sure I'll be needing one. Better keep it for yourself. You sure as hell will need it before we're through with you and your prisoner. Any special favors you have been granting him will soon be stopped. You'll be looking for another job. Find yourself a nondescript job in an out of the way place. Even so, it may not be nondescript enough!"

"I take that as a direct threat, Grady."

"Then you read me right! Now push that goddamned button and let me out of here."

"Sure." He pushed the buzzer, the door opened. "Harry! Escort the Assistant DA out." It had only been a couple of minutes later that he heard Harry yelling.

Anderson sighed, "There will be hell to pay for this accident." He opened the door to his office, picked up the phone and called Jacob. "Sorry Skipper, we've had a slight hitch in our plans. Grady Beal is seriously injured from a fall down the steps. He may not live."

"What? Who did it?"

"That's the weird part—nobody did it. According to Harry, he lost his footing and fell. Nobody was anywhere near him when it happened. It really was an accident."

Jacob thought to himself that someone sure was slick. What he said was, "Now that's a real surprise. Do you think that will be one less or one more problem to worry about?"

" I do feel sorry for his children. They're the ones who will have a rough time emotionally. If he dies, his insurance plus what Melissa found out he has in the bank plus what he has probably stashed at home should send them all to college."

Warden Anderson scratched his ear. "Only time will tell on that one, Jacob. Meanwhile, you'd better stay out of sight. You'll be the first person they will suspect. Since Harry saw it all, I sent him to fax a statement to the DA and to the press stating exactly what happened."

"Under the circumstances, do you think that's wise?"

"I had to tell him we know he's a snitch to the DA. I explained that once that fax is sent, then the DA can't make him change his testimony. It seemed a good compromise to both of us."

"Piece of very special cake, Warden. You're one smart man. It was best for Harry. I could tear him apart on the stand as any good prosecutor would. Does any of this change your mind about our plans?"

"No! It just makes it easier on my conscience. Beal was a follower, not a leader."

"Are you going to your Mason meeting tonight?"

"Always do."

"I want to send something to Rayford Hammond."

"Anything in it that I should know about?"

"With my permission, you can open it and read it."

Anderson laughed and waved Jacob out.

"I'd rather not know. I've had enough for one day. I'll send a guard to get it."

Chapter 16

A rmond Barfus couldn't believe that Grady Beal was in the hospital so badly injured that he probably wouldn't live until morning. But it was true. The phone slipped from his sweaty palm to land with a thud on the wood floor. Had it been Jacob? How could it be? He would have been in a cell at the prison. He stooped down to pick up the phone.

"Did Anderson see him fall?"

"No! He said they talked about parole for Ford James and Jacob Reynolds, then Grady left. The guard, Harry Malone, was the only one who saw Grady fall. You know Harry's our guy at the prison. He said no one was near Grady when he fell. Damned SOB even made a statement to the press that it was an accident."

"Did Anderson tell you what Beal said about Jacob's parole?"

"There was no discussion on that subject. Anderson called to let me know what happened. Grady was already at the hospital by the time he got through to me."

"Has Grady's wife been notified?"

"Yes, she's at the hospital now."

"Okay! The news media has been notified and will probably be at the hospital, so be prepared."

It was just like the colonel to be thinking of publicity, not the injured man; always the politics, and Dan Hollis was very annoyed. Grady had been a good man, a family man.

Only one reporter and a photographer were at the

hospital when Dan Hollis pulled into a parking space twenty minutes later. "Mr. Hollis, do you think Grady Beal's fall was an accident as Harry Malone stated?" a reporter asked.

"According to Harry, it was an unfortunate accident. However, we will investigate until fully satisfied that this is indeed the case." His face showed sincere concern; he wanted to be damned sure that Grady wasn't talking out of his head.

When Beal's wife, Susan, saw him she ran into his arms like a child. "He's going to die! Oh, Dan, we're losing him!"

Dan asked the nurse if she could get a sedative for Grady's wife. When Susan was finally calmed down, with a neighbor holding her hand, he went to find Dr. Brantley to get an update on Grady's condition.

At the nurses station, Hollis asked, "Is Dr. Brantley here?"

"Yes sir. He's down the hall in number thirty-five. If you'll wait just a minute, I'll tell him you're here."

"Never mind, I'll find him myself." Dan Hollis didn't want to wait that long. He walked as quickly down the hall as his gimp leg would allow. He took the doctor by the arm and led him away from the nurses. "I have a 'need to know' situation here, Bill. Give it to me straight about Grady."

"Get your pinstripe pressed, Dan, you'll be needing it. He won't last the night. You want the details?"

"No! I'll read your report. I have to ask . . . has he said anything at all?"

"He was in a coma when he arrived and that condition isn't likely to change. He isn't talking, if that's what you mean. He's too far gone for that. We've called in a neurosurgeon, Dr. Simmons. Grady's brain is swelling, and we're taking him to surgery, but he's already technically dead and will be paralyzed from the neck down if he lives. Susan has signed the forms to take him off life-support and donate any organs for transplant should he become brain dead. I can tell you right now he is technically dead already. Do you think foul play was involved?"

"Not at all. Harry Malone was there and saw Grady fall. Apparently it was one of those unavoidable accidents. He's a damned fine man, Doctor. Do everything you can for him."

"It's already being done."

Dan Hollis walked back up the hallway. He wasn't dumb; something wasn't right. His professional reasoning could smell it, but there was no way Grady would ever tell him anything. Besides, Harry was his man at the prison, and Harry was the main witness to the fall. Just an unfortunate accident or a well-planned murder? Jacob Reynolds again? No way he could have done it in front of Harry — or could he?

He pulled a cell phone from his pocket and unfolded it and punched in a number. "I want a full investigation of the accident at the prison this morning. I want those stairs gone over with a fine-tooth comb! Work on the possibility that this wasn't accidental. I know what Harry said he saw! Just do the sweep and report all findings to me, whatever the hour."

Armond Barfus answered Dan's call on the first ring.

"I've seen Grady. He's in a coma, unable to talk."

"Will he live?"

"They're operating, but it appears hopeless."

"Well, start looking for a replacement we can use. Until you find one, let Giddy Smith assist you. We'll handle our own affairs."

"Giddy Smith! Hell, Arm! I'll get fire from all sides on that. He's just too damn controversial. He was mentioned in that pornography trial. He may be your man but he leaves carrion in his wake! The public hates him!"

"The public be damned! This is my town. Giddy knows his way around."

"You know his reputation and you still want him? Come on, Arm, reconsider — that could ruin us all."

"He was never convicted of anything. His name

simply came up in a court case is all. He's our man and this will give him a chance to get respectable. I have to catch an airplane in one hour. I'm counting on you to handle this and settle Giddy temporarily in Grady's job."

A cold chill rolled down Dan Hollis' back. Giddy provided Arm with his young stuff — their well-kept secret, or so they thought. How had he let Armond Barfus talk him into this? That goddamned money just wasn't worth the stress, especially now that accidents were starting again.

He limped to his car, saw his driver talking with several fellow policemen beside the steps. He glanced up and down the street, whistled for his driver, and then he saw the tire. It was totally flat.

"I'll wait in the cafeteria," he told the driver, then turned and reentered the hospital. He went to the cafeteria and poured himself a cup of coffee, his hand shaking so the coffee sloshed out, staining the cuff of his white shirtsleeve. He reminded himself over and over that Jacob Reynolds was in prison.

He sat at a table with his back to the wall. So far Bo was the only one working on Jacob's case that had not had any trouble. He could not understand why they were all being so screwed over and nothing ever happened to Bo! Since it was Bo's case if Jacob was set on revenge, he would go after Bo first, or would he? Or did he know that Barfus had set Bo up to take the fall? The man was an enigma.

Reynolds would have to be a stone-cold killer to have gotten Beal in front of Malone. How the shit could all this happen with him never even on the scene? In the past he had thought there must be a gang, but he had checked out all the men who worked at the warehouse and found they were family men, all old, fifty and over. So they were all vets, so were a lot of World War II servicemen and they never brought their war skills home with them. Apathy of the voting public had been their trump card but what would happen when Giddy Smith came into the picture?

District Attorney Dan Hollis shifted his weight off his

bad hip. A flash of his own accident that afternoon in
June, almost three years ago, ran through his mind. He
had gone to the farm to exercise his stallion, Midnight.
They were ready to clear the last jump, something they
had done hundreds of times on the obstacle course. He
remembered the sweet smell of pine trees in the air, the
newly mowed grass, the sweat of the horse, the powerful
muscles running full out toward the jump. Then
Midnight's head came up in a magnificent shake of his
mane, of fright, then he shied and the feeling of flying
from the saddle, trying to roll to absorb the impact,
slamming into the ground, one hip hitting a downed tree
limb, shattering the ball from the socket, breaking his leg.
The stunned silence that followed, with only the bees
buzzing, the horse snorting, then the pain hit and he
couldn't move. Several operations later the doctors finally
gave him the bad news. Although the hip had healed, it
would always be weak; he would have to favor it and be
careful. Possibly, he could avoid a hip replacement. He
still needed to use a crutch.

Was it something Jacob had done to spook that reliable
horse? Or was it actually something in the grass? Would
he ever know the truth? If the accidents were beginning
again even more violently, he would get out. He could
practice law somewhere else. No way was he ever going
to go through that again, certainly not for Colonel Barfus —
most certainly not painted with the same brush that stained
Giddy Smith.

"Sir! Your car is ready. It was a nail in the tire, sir — a
big one. As a matter of fact, there were two flats. I borrowed
another spare. It was probably from the construction last
week."

That was a sensible deduction, but in his bones, Dan
knew better. It had never stopped — not in the two years
since they had sent Jacob Reynolds to prison. Could it be
Jacob's way of telling him that what happened to Beal was
not an accident?

Chapter 17

Dan remembered that weekend in September clearly: the cool breezes, the hot sun and perfect rippling ocean currents, the gentle rocking of the boat lulling him to sleep on the prime, highly polished deck. He, Ancell Dart and Phil Williams had anchored Phil's yacht off the Carolina coast. A pretty girl he had wanted to get alone for some time was a guest, along with a couple of other beauties.

He was excited, expectant; he just didn't know how Phil would arrange the liaison. He hated to admit to himself even now that he had been firecracker hot at the prospect of having that young woman to himself. As it turned out, he did get to touch her, but not in the way he had intended. She was passed out and lay on the bed before him, dressed only in a tiny bikini. Just as he walked to the bed, he heard Dart yell his name. Walking out into the corridor, he saw Ancell frantically motioning him to hurry.

Entering Phil Williams' berth, he saw the other three young ladies lined up on the bed, also still dressed in their bikinis, sound asleep.

"Not there, you fool! Here!" Dart was pointing to a crumpled heap that was Phil Williams on the floor. He stooped down, took hold of the silk pajama top at the shoulder and rolled the man over. He gasped at the expression of horror on the dead man's face. The first thought that flew through his mind was that it would take a skilled mortician or a closed casket for this one. Clutched in Phil's hand was an asthma spray bottle. Dan took a napkin and removed it, holding it at arm's length; he sure as hell wasn't going to take a whiff.

He looked around, bent down to feel the carpet; it was damp near the steps, which were wiped clean, leaving only a trace of dampness but no footprints. It didn't take a genius to realize that Phil had not died of natural causes. Someone had been on the boat, had seen them all and knew that all the girls had been drugged. Evidently Phil and Ancell had been doing this for a long time. Now, someone else knew what they were doing, and Dan was caught right smack in the middle between murder, drugs and rape! That alone should have sent him packing. Instead he had moved the women to the deck, straightened Phil out in the bed, tried to manipulate the muscles in his face and closed his eyes. Then he opened a fresh bottle of asthma medication, curled the dead man's fingers around the bottle, leaving it there, and had thrown the other one overboard.

He poured a strong brandy for Ancell and a vodka for himself. "You skulking worm! What have you gotten me tied into? How long have you two been doing this?"

"Hell, Dan, we thought you'd be pleased. You've been talking about Connie for months! How was I to know he'd die of an asthma attack." Ancell's hand shook, causing the brandy to slosh in the glass. The man was in shock.

"Drink that goddamned brandy, you're going into shock! Look at his face, Ancell. He saw something that put that expression there and it wasn't an asthma-induced heart attack! He's been murdered! Not only that but I have to cover it up and become an accessory to that murder! My being here implicates me, and a number of people saw me here. How could you both do this without realizing there would be a day of reckoning? Granted I have taken your money and I have pulled strings that should have been cut, but taking a bribe is nothing compared to what you two have been doing. Pull yourself together, you're going to help me carry those girls in when we get back. We don't have to call about Phil until we want to just as long as we have our stories straight. I'm going to get us some coffee then I'm going to take her to dock and you had better be ready to help!"

Later, totally exhausted, he had returned to the sloop, showered and changed clothes. Gulping down a vodka, feeling it burn all the way down, he waited, thinking that whoever had done the job probably had taken pictures and would try to blackmail Ancell or even himself. If—no not *if*—*when* they did, he'd find the bastard and take him out.

The coroner's report was death by asthma induced heart attack. Evidently that had been the killer's plan and it had worked perfectly. Now he was a party to Ancell Dart's evil, as well as helping the killer cover up his crime. Actually, he didn't blame the assassin, but Dart's and Williams' stupidity, thinking with the little head.

That had been three months ago. In his office, leaning forward in his big chair now, he reviewed his part in Jacob Reynolds' destruction, knowing that was when it all started. Did Jacob hire someone to hit Phil Williams? No blackmailing letter had been received but the killer could be waiting for a more appropriate time, saving it as insurance should he be arrested. Who really wanted to destroy Jacob? All of a sudden it didn't make sense. None of the men involved had even known the man before they had set him up to be disbarred. Why Reynolds? He drew a blank. None of them had been in Vietnam. None had grown up with Jacob. Not even Martin Long, who came from Savannah—or did he? Why had he never questioned Barfus about Long? The vicious way Barfus had raped the Hull girl, even after she sold herself to frame Jacob, was inhuman. He grimaced at the memory. Another warning he had failed to heed. The total weight of his sellout settled like a dark cowl on his soul, which had become far too heavy to carry any longer. The colonel was totally out of control, wanting him to take on Giddy Smith. The nerve of the man!

He laughed, a bitter frustrated laugh. Damn you, Jacob. You're a demon. Hating you makes me disgusted with myself and with what I have become. What I have done to Grady Beal and to myself. Was I ever good? Looking back he saw a poor kid who lucked up with a college scholarship and went to law school. He had been

seduced by the money—more money than he had ever
seen in his life. Everybody does it, don't they? Who the
hell is honest anymore? Certainly no one I know. Then
why am I feeling guilty? Show me a judge with integrity.
Hell, if Ancell was arrested for rape his only loss would
be the time and money spent and a slap at his reputation.
Not so for him; if he were implicated it would mean his
reputation and loss of career. Now he knew there was
only one way to handle the situation. He sat down to
dictate paperwork recommending parole for Jacob Denton
Reynolds. Maybe this would clear him with Jacob, maybe
not, for the man would be free but still unable to practice
law. Releasing Jacob would be damage control for the
moment, and if Jacob were the guilty party it would look
to Jacob that he had gotten the message and paid them
back for his part in the disbarment proceedings. If he was
wrong, more trouble would be forthcoming. He didn't
think his relationship with Barfus could be traced, or the
bribe money now that Grady was dead. The shit was
about to hit the fan and if he didn't make a move soon he
would be right under it. Dan took out his phone to call
Smith. He had worked with Smith several times, but
pulling him into the vacuum created by Beal's accident
would expose that relationship.

He stopped in mid-dial. The closure of resignation
came suddenly, giving him a feeling of peace he had not
known since his association with Barfus had begun. For
the first time he really realized that he was fighting for his
life. Life would still be good if he had not been so greedy,
he finally admitted to himself.

Harry Malone, the prison guard, had set the example:
go public before you can be stopped. The colonel was out
of town on a case for a week; by the time he returned it
would all be over. Buzzing his secretary, Dan left word he
was not to be disturbed. With a sigh, he opened his laptop
and started his letter of resignation, stating as the cause,
his injury and the demands of the job. Jacob had destroyed
his career without firing a shot.

Chapter 18

Counselor Armond Barfus wore a self-satisfied smirk on his well tanned, deeply lined face as he drove in from the airport. Even the treacherous resignation by his DA, Dan Hollis, didn't faze him. He had called Elizabeth, his wife, to meet him; he wanted to go to the club and celebrate his well won multi-million settlement in the Clement case. Instead, there was a message that she had left his car with the valet service. He was annoyed, but not angry. Liz wasn't the woman she once was.

For several years they had been going their separate ways; she had not been interested in sex for years, spending most of her time at Emory, taking a class or two but mostly doing charity work. For the first time, he wondered why she spent so much time there. He had been so involved with his own life—and women—that he now realized it had been years since he had seen her except for Wednesday nights and Sunday mornings. He spent all his time at the club with his friends or on the golf course.

Turning into his driveway through the stone gateway, he found his way impeded by a mound of boxes, suitcases and trunks. Unable to avoid them, he braked to a stop and got out of his car. A uniformed guard was standing beside the items. "I'm Colonel Barfus, I live here. What is all this stuff?"

The guard stood in a relaxed position, hands behind his back. "These are your things, sir. You are to get them off the property immediately. I was told to give you this." He handed Barfus the papers he had been holding behind his back.

Realization slowly sank in. He only read the beginning of the papers, seeing the name of Jack Wold, a well-known divorce barrister, and he knew he was in trouble. Taking his phone he dialed Giddy Smith. Smith told him he would get a van and be there in thirty minutes. While he waited, it began to rain again. Cursing, his dignity bruised beyond belief, he began to load what he recognized as most valuable into his car. The guard stood back under an umbrella. Barfus barked at him, "The least you could do is help me load these things."

"I don't work for you, sir. Moving this much personal luggage is not in my job description. Counselor Wold said to tell you the rest of your belongings were sent to the house at Gadby."

By the time Giddy arrived, the boxes and trunks were soaking wet. "Take them to the apartment on Riverside, Giddy. I'm going to my office. I'll meet you there around eleven."

Calling Liz's personal number only resulted in a message that she was out of town.

The rain was a steady downpour as he drove to his office. In the executive bathroom, he showered, then put on clean clothes. Since it was after nine p.m., no one was in the building but the night watchman. Fuming, Barfus stood staring out the window, drinking a brandy, and trying to decide on a course of action. Liz had actually kicked him out. One doesn't kick someone of his stature out, but that was exactly what she had done.

The phone rang. The security guard was calling to tell him a Jack Wold was downstairs. "Send the bastard up."

There was a loud knock on his office door. He unlocked the door for Jack. "May I come in?"

"I'd sooner entertain the devil himself."

Jack walked in along with another man who looked like a hired bodyguard. "Apparently you got the papers."

"Yes, how thoughtful of you to handle everything so

graciously."

Jack smiled. "I suppose I would feel the same. I just wanted you to know that you are to leave Liz completely alone. That is her request and I would hate to have to get an injunction. She prefers as little publicity as possible and surely you agree."

"Why should I want to hide a divorce?"

"You should know that my client has sold all the stock in her name." Armond Barfus actually dropped his drink. "She's asking for all the property in her name. The only reason you were able to get in here today is you returned early. The locks will be changed tomorrow."

For a second Barfus stood in shocked surprise. "You'll be in hell before that happens, Jack!"

"In that case, I'll see you in court. Until then do not go to the house, it belongs exclusively to Liz. If you decide to contest, here are copies of Snoop Magazine which will hit the newsstands this weekend—along with several very interesting pictures Snoop has not yet published. Copies of the originals of your little redheaded minor, along with her statements about what happened when she was fourteen, are in a safe place. Other copies have been sent to the Governor. I suggest you quietly retire. You'll still receive your 10 percent of the yearly receipts from your own stock in the firm."

Barfus leaned heavily on the desk. "Jack, when did all this happen?" Liz had given him no inkling she was planning such a move, nor had he thought she was even capable when he had left the previous Monday. He shuddered to think of all the other stock he had put in her name, some of which was in his secret vault. Many times he had thought to show it to Liz, but was grateful now that he had not. Yet he could do nothing without her signature. Had she actually known what she was signing? She had paid so little attention to business and seemed so annoyed by it all.

He still had the account in Switzerland. Liz did not know about that and fortunately the papers were not at the office. It would be more than sufficient for anyone to retire comfortably. Only, he did not like losing. All this ran through his mind in an instant.

"Where did she get the pictures?" He looked expectantly at Jack, all the while grateful that at least they didn't know about the girl he had raped and that Ancell had paid her two hundred thousand to frame Jacob.

"Liz received the pictures in the mail. Then the next day as a courtesy to Liz, the magazine sent her a proof of what was to be printed. That was about two weeks ago. Well, I came to tell you as professional courtesy, but from now on it will all be work."

"Do I thank the devil or kill him?"

"I'm not doing anything you wouldn't do and you know it, Barfus. If the tables were turned, I wouldn't have gotten this courtesy call."

"Right! Thanks but I'll fight you, as you well know."

"Won't work, Arm. You're caught red-handed—or redheaded, shall we say. You should have kept your women of legal age—and your men. Man, you blew it in more ways than one. There's also an investigation concerning your role in the disbarment of Jacob Reynolds. It seems you played more than a little part in that scheme."

Barfus was aghast. He fully understood the implications; any future he may have left would be in prison. Only one person could have sent those pictures and there was no doubt it was Marge. I'll find her and kill her with my own hands, he thought, losing awareness that Jack was even still there. He was surprised when Jack spoke.

"Liz came to me two weeks ago with the pictures and the statements. We've worked every day since. She's a brilliant woman. I wasn't aware that she was in the legal profession."

Armond just stood there with his mouth open. "What are you talking about? Liz's only connection to the legal profession is through me."

"She passed the bar with flying colors while you were

gone. Not only that, her L.L.B. in criminal law will serve her well at Town and Allen."

So all the charity work wasn't charity at all. Why the sneaky little bitch! The idea of his private life being wagged before his eyes shocked him so that his mind wouldn't focus.

"Who will represent you, Arm?" Jack was watching a brilliant attorney fall apart. Suddenly, Colonel Armond Barfus was changing. The jaunty in-control man he had seen when he walked in was gone, his shoulders slumped, his face seemed to fall apart.

"I'll have to let you know. Ben Tremont, probably."

"Arm, we've known each other a lot of years and in the kind of life you've led, maybe you don't quite realize yet that criminal charges will be filed. Not only on the Rasher girl but the Hull affair as well." The shock of that revelation buckled Barfus' knees and he sat down heavily in the nearest chair.

"Arm, you need to listen to more gossip. Annabelle Livingston, the federal prosecutor, and Jacob have been close friends for a long time. She did the investigation and filed all the evidence. I don't know why you took Jacob on, but it was a huge mistake. You aren't in his class."

With that statement, Wold walked out, closing the door behind him.

Chapter 19

The sleek black Chrysler, its darkly tinted windows mirroring the brick row houses, moved quietly down the narrow street, slowly coming to a stop. The driver squinted to see down the shadowed alleyway, checking to see if it was blocked. Then he maneuvered the car through discarded beer cans and fast food wrappers to a parking lot behind a long brick building, a landmark bar that, like many others, had lost its dignity when the in-crowd moved on to trendy Buckhead. Barfus remembered going there as a college student and a tingling of regret was quickly checked by uncontrollable anger.

A stream of foul greasy water ran through the asphalt parking lot from a large refuge container. Barfus hesitated before stepping onto the pavement, checking his back-trail to see if he had been followed. Then he turned on the car alarm. If he lost this car, he couldn't call the police.

Wearing a black wig, sunglasses and a green plaid coat, he hoped no one would recognize him from the newspaper photographs. He walked around to the front of the restaurant and opened the door to a dingy smoke-filled room. An antique bar covered one wall, its soft pallor of aged wood waxed to a high sheen. The old wooden stools were scuffed and worn, yet the brass rails still shone from much polishing. Originally the place had been built by a sea captain wanting to get far away from the water. The place served seafood and steaks that were still the best in town, but it was now located in a lonely and desolate area long forgotten by the elite.

Choice of a meeting place had been set by the man,

Mitchell. Barfus looked with disgust at the scarred tile floor and faded curtains. He took a booth in the back and ordered a bourbon. The young black waiter returned with the drink and asked if he wanted anything else.

"I'm Mr. Smith and I'm waiting for a Mr. Mitchell."

"Yes, sir! He said you'd be here. He's on his way."

Barfus didn't expect to see anyone he knew, but he didn't want Mitchell pushing the price higher just because he was wanted by the law. He was looking out the window watching the street when he felt the table move. He looked around to see a big black man sit down across the table from him. He had the busted nose and cauliflower ears of a former boxer — obviously not a successful one. He now made his living hitting from behind and was for hire.

"You the man, Smith?"

"Yes, I recognize you, Mitchell. I remember when you were a fighter. Are you as mean as they say?"

"Meaner than *they* will ever know, if you get my drift."

Barfus slid an envelope across the table. "That's the only picture of her I could find; fifty copies as you requested and one-third of the money. Soon as you find her, I want to know where she is, then we'll decide what to do. Don't do anything foolish; don't let her know she's been found."

"How do I reach you?"

Barfus thought for a minute, then said. "I'll meet you here next week at the same time. If you have the information, I'll send for your money."

"All I have to do is find the woman?" Mitchell was surprised; usually he was asked to do much more.

"That's all for now. Meet me here even if you haven't found her and report what you have done."

The big black man moved his two hundred and eighty pounds out of the booth. "All right then, I'll see you next week, same time, same place." Mitchell laughed as he left, talking to his sidekick, Skinny. "That white bastard Barfus trying to disguise himself. Nobody with that high a profile can hide behind a hat and a wig. That fucker's desperate." He didn't say aloud that after he got the fifty big ones, he would shake Barfus down for all he had.

The rest of the day Mitchell distributed the pictures to his family and friends. Then he cruised the strip asking the girls if they had seen Marge. In every direction he drew a blank. The woman had never been on the street. He cruised in his black Cadillac using his car-phone to check everyone he knew, and he checked all the bars.

Driving away from the bar, Barfus reviewed what he would do. *Preeminent* was what Maurice Thompson had said the morning he resigned. Something about Jacob Reynolds' nickname in Vietnam. He had told them they were opening a Pandora's box. He had thought the young man ignorant to question their influence and power. Aloud, he reviewed what had happened: "Two of my oldest clients are dead. One partner's in a mental institution and one retired due to stress. The district attorney that I owned resigned on public television, and I must not forget Grady Beal is dead. Jacob Reynolds is released from prison and will probably be coming after me — but first, I'll get Marge!"

Only Marge could have taken the pictures that destroyed him. He had been wary when she disappeared so suddenly. He'd had Maggie at the time, so he hadn't missed her. He should have been alarmed instead of curious. He couldn't go after Maggie, having found out she was being closely guarded. He ground his fist into his temple. "No little bitch gets the best of me!" His mind settled on Marge and he believed it had been she who had destroyed his future as Governor, maybe even President! He would soon be disbarred, his life ruined! All because of her!

It never occurred to Barfus, suffering in the backlash of his own sick excesses, that he was to blame because he could not accept that his problems were of his own design. In his denial, he focused on Marge, knowing she had to be the one who had taken the pictures. When Mitchell found her, he would kill her! He'd blow her fucking head off! In his unbridled hate, in the dark recesses of his sick mind, Barfus found a target for his own destructive mistakes.

Chapter 20

Marge stepped quietly into the barn and Boom said, "Well, are you just going to stand there watching or do you intend to help?"

"I didn't think you knew I was here," she replied.

"The light changed when you walked in — it got brighter."

Boom pulled the halter over the Tennessee Walker's ears and watched Marge carrying the small English saddle to the tack room. Since her arrival, Boom realized he had found more than a cure for his loneliness. Her spontaneity, affection and willingness to learn was like a child seeing the world for the first time. He supposed he was stupid to have fallen absolutely in love. She was young enough to be his daughter. She walked back, reaching for the bridle, and he caught her hand. "Marry me, Marge!" That's all he could say, looking into those big blue eyes, knowing but innocent for all her experience, for he suspected love was something she had not had a lot of in her lifetime.

"Boom, you don't know what you're saying! You don't know anything about me, where I've been or what I've done. If you did you would hate me, not love me."

"Why don't you tell me all about your life and let me decide for myself."

The dam opened and for the rest of the day the total sum of her life rolled out in a flood of emotion, ending with her liaison with Jacob. Boom held her, dried her tears, fed her coffee and encouraged her to talk. He simply ignored her protestations that she would not be good for his reputation. "I'm an independent man, Marge. I don't cater to public opinion. I'm not a politician, nor a cleric; I love you, I enjoy your company, you please me in a way no one ever has simply by being here, by being yourself. Unless you find me disagreeable, let's get married."

Any further protest by her was lost as he silenced her with a kiss. Every other man in her life, she now knew, had been nothing but sexual exercise. Even her evening with Jacob, as much fun as it had been, didn't qualify. To have love and sex together was a totally new and indescribably beautiful experience.

She was nobody's fool, knowing that most good things in her life eventually disappeared. Her father had died of an overdose. She had loved him dearly. Her mother married again and her stepfather had raped and abused her, so she had run away. At thirteen she was on the streets, on her own, on the run, and lost. The day she arrived with only one small suitcase, she had met Giddy Smith. He wasn't even looking for a girl, but saw her and the suitcase and he parked to talk. She allowed him to pay for a room, with the stipulation that he would not bother her but let her have time to think. He agreed. He had brought his sixteen-year-old friend to talk with her and explain what he wanted.

What she heard was better than what she had left. He paid her well and treated her with respect. He also taught her things she did not want to know. He put her up in a small neat apartment, which didn't make up for what she was coerced into doing. She stayed his girl for two years, saving every penny of her weekly 'salary'.

When he found a still younger girl, he bought her a small condo as a going-away present. She knew it was hush money. They remained friends for years. He was weird, but not mean and he was clean. Somehow he made a girl want to please him. It was still wrong, but better than all the rest. So when he asked her to *take care* of friends who paid her well, she fell into the mold that he had learned worked well.

She decided then that no one would touch her unless she wanted them. She had held to it until she met the colonel. Refusing him had been difficult, because he made it so. He hired an investigator to give him a report on her, and found out about her sister. She appealed to Giddy Smith, who refused to help, only telling her the colonel would pay her sister enough to set up her own place.

She left that night; it had been two years since she had seen her sister. Her sister was only eleven years old. Giddy had told her that the reason her stepfather had not yet bothered the girl was that he had just put her on the market and that he, Giddy, had decided to buy her and sell her to Armond Barfus.

She had left Giddy's and driven straight to her old home and snatched Millie. The next day they drove to a private school in Maryland. She had explained the problem in order to get the Mother Superior to accept her sister into the Catholic boarding school. No way would she have her little sister suffer her own fate. The only problem had been Barfus. He had threatened to find Millie. Marge had not known if he could, but he was so powerful she had agreed to his demands.

The first time he had become violent she picked up a chair and would have bashed his head in, but he suddenly changed tactics and never again threatened her. Had she not fought back it would have been a different story. In her limited worldly innocence, even she could see he had a cruel, cowardly bent to his character.

There was a deep betrayal, knowing that her own mother had known she was being abused and had even helped hold her down, and watched, stoned out of her mind. So, Marge was satisfied with her decision to give Jacob the pictures of the colonel. She had taken them to protect herself should he ever threaten her again.

Now Boom had come into her life, offering a life of security beyond her wildest dreams. She was accepted by his buddies and their families, yet she feared that she would wake up one day and *poof*, it would all be gone, and she would be homeless again; yet she knew that if anything happened to Boom, Jacob Reynolds would take care of her as long as he was alive. But Jacob was always in danger. She tried to shake off the uneasy feeling that had nagged at her all morning.

Boom was watching the play of emotions on her face. Seeing the horror and pain that she constantly covered up, he put his arms around her and held her. "Get used to the idea, Marge, we're going to be married and soon." The lemon scent in her hair, the softness of her body brought forth a sigh. "You can't imagine the peace I feel just now, the contentment. In some ways it scares me, the old guilt complex I suppose, wondering how I deserved to live long enough to experience this kind of happiness. Knowing the caprice of life, I savor the moment. I want to make time stand still so nothing will change, and that what we have together will go on forever."

"It will, Boom, I promise you, it will. I love you with all my heart."

Boom felt the vibration of the phone and resented the intrusion, but he was expecting a call from the governor. Unfolding the phone, he said, "Ellenberg here!"

It was Irish. "Boom! D.R. is out! The DA did all the paperwork before he left office. Annabelle is bringing him home. We're on our way there to get everything ready. Bring some beer, it's time to celebrate!"

"Beer hell! That's Champagne news!" He turned to Marge. "D.R.'s been released."

"Do you think it had anything to do with your contribution to the governor's campaign fund?"

"Why you little sneak, how did you know that?"

"Little pitchers have big ears. Race you to the house. I feel like taking a shower — want to wash my back?"

"That's an offer I can't refuse!"

Chapter 21

Annabelle breathed a sigh of relief as the G-4 executive jet touched down on the runway at Hartsfield International. Two hours later she was back in her office making phone calls, then she left for Sanborn Prison to pick up Jacob.

It had been a harried but successful trip. As the new acting district attorney, it had been her first priority, the only catch being that she had to give the women immunity from prosecution. That was acceptable in order to get the real culprits, Armond Barfus and Goren Thomas. Only her assistant had not yet located either man.

It still amazed her what people would do for money. According to the girl, she had consented to the rape for a hundred thousand, her aunt getting another hundred thousand; however, what she received wasn't worth the money. She had not expected to be beaten so severely that she would be scarred for life. Annabelle felt some compassion for the girl who would suffer the consequences all her life. No amount of money was worth that kind of pain. She had her statements, witnessed and sealed along with photographs of the women and had faxed certified copies to the governor, asking for immediate release of Jacob Reynolds, along with his reinstatement to the Bar. She had sent copies of all the information to George Markman at the CIA. She suspected that the information she had uncovered involved drug money, and that it was involved in and out of the country, which was out of her jurisdiction.

Annabelle was a happy woman when she walked into

Warden Anderson's office and handed him the Governor's signed release papers personally. "Sit down, Annabelle, this is a great day. I knew he was innocent. Anyone who knew Reynolds would know he couldn't have done anything like that."

Anderson turned to the guard, "Harry, get Jacob Reynolds." Turning back to Annabelle, he said, "You're probably going to find a lot of problems in that office. I have a few others you may want to look into."

"This job is going to take some straightening out. It seems the filing system is long past needing updating, and scrutinizing. There are some files in a mass of boxes supposedly never to be found. I have three friends helping straighten it out."

Jacob came in grinning. "Well, pretty lady, what are you doing in my hotel?"

"Thought I'd come by and see if you had time to go to Marty's on the square for lunch."

"Congratulations! I hear you're the new acting DA."

"Dean and Maurice pushed that, said I was what was needed, an honest woman."

"It won't be an easy job, Annabelle."

"Maybe not, but so far a satisfying one. Take a look at these documents!"

"Jacob studied the papers thrust into his hands as a slow grin burst into laughter. "I'll be a son of a gun! You did it! You actually did it! By God! Even to a confession."

"I didn't have any choice. My Saturday nights were dull as hell, not to mention the weekdays." Tears were streaming down her cheeks. "Damn, look at me, the hard-as-nails district attorney, crying. Doesn't that beat all!" Jacob put his arms tighter around her, with her head on his shoulder and held her while she sobbed. "Dammit! D.R., I've missed you something fierce."

"Honey, if only you knew. We'll make up for it later; you'd better believe it. Can we go now?"

"Just need to sign a few papers. Now, get out of here! I'll bring your stuff to you. I'll see you in town."

"Anderson, when you have time go through your own files, let me know any you think are here due to the previous administration's manipulations," Annabelle said when Jacob had left. "I can't promise anything but an honest evaluation."

"That's all anyone could ask, Annabelle."

Walking out of the prison, Jacob trembled, partly from the emotion of again being free, but also from the anger of being falsely imprisoned for two long years. Driving into town he got a call from Boom. "We'll meet you all at the cabin! Don't worry, we won't stay long." They could hear Marge laughing in the background.

"D.R., I found a direct connection between Barfus, Phil Williams, Ancell Dart, Grady Beal and Dan Hollis . . . and a man named Goren Thomas. I get the inkling that Thomas is the key to it all. There are other people in with him but I don't have any names. The mud gets thinner as you walk outward, but it stinks just as bad."

Annabelle was driving so she didn't see the flicker of shocked recognition, followed by anger, pull Jacob's face into a scowl. She was telling him all the details of the Hull women's confession. "It seems a man that Mamie Hull once knew as a teenager paid them. It was Thomas. Do you know anything about him? He was in Vietnam, but there is little information on him since that time. He may be the Martin Long who was seen with Barfus a time or two and with whom he had business dealings. Do you know the man?"

Did he know Goren Thomas? Does a Christian know about the Devil? Now everything that had happened made sense — not just sense, but cause for what had been done to him. He would rather Annabelle didn't know because he would seek his own revenge, so he said, "There were so many over there. I'd have to see his photograph to remember."

Annabelle continued, "The CIA found that two men by the name, Goren Thomas, have used passports recently. Both are still out of the country. They found accounts in the name of Goren Thomas in seven banks. It was there that they found the connection to Martin Long. Goren Thomas may be Martin Long. More searching of Armond Barfus' files showed a host of connections. Martin Long was a partner in two construction developments along with Ancell Dart and Phil Williams. Phil Williams is dead and Ancell Dart is hospitalized for mental instability.

"There were six accounts under the name of Martin Long in Charlotte, North Carolina. That's where they hit paydirt. Martin Long's last address was in Atlanta. The accounts of Goren Thomas and Martin Long were an investigator's dream of checks payable to companies they are looking into for connections to known drug dealers all over the country — many written for construction work and financial consultation, investments and management of four resorts. One in Spain, one in France and two in Africa. That's all I know about. Where do you want to go?"

"Just take me home."

"Okay. Your friends Bulldozer and Johnny were going up there this morning to be sure everything was okay. They should still be there. They've planned a welcoming home party for you. I hope you don't mind."

"Hell, no! I could use one myself."

George had been watching developments in the Jacob Reynolds case for over a year, ever since Mark Douglas had given him Jacob's resume. He was talking to one of his field men in Nashville at the same time Annabelle was driving Jacob home.

Whoever he sent to go after Goren Thomas needed to be someone outside the system. It was obvious Thomas had listening posts within every organization. He had withdrawn the money from his accounts within thirty minutes after they had gotten that information. Why not send Jacob? He wanted to work for the Agency. Give him a chance, he certainly would be dedicated to the job.

George laughed. It certainly would serve Goren Thomas right. Sometimes justice had its brighter side.

He turned to his assistant. "Billy Joe, I have a special assignment for you. You are to talk with no one within any organization about this. I know you have been itching to get into the field again."

Driving up to the cabin, pine needles and leaves blowing in the storm, sticking to the car only to be washed away with the next deluge, Jacob found himself home. Smoke curled in a narrow stream from the chimney, only to be immediately dissipated by the wind. They were all there: Bulldozer, Zelda and their five boys, Marge and Boom, Irish and Mary and their three-month-old twins. Even Jason and Sarah were there.

Later, as everyone was leaving, Boom walked up to D.R. and handed him a key. "Remember that cabin I bought on Fort Mountain? Why don't you take some time off and do a little R&R. Great view, stocked library, fully stocked kitchen and bar. Little Lion and his wife live in the guesthouse. Make it your home away from home. Give you time to think and plan what you want to do with nobody knowing where you are."

"Thanks, Boom, I think I'll take you up on that. Don't let anyone come up here while I'm gone. I saw the papers, so will Goren, and he knows where to find me. I've already warned my daughter. Her mother has taken her to France to get immersed in the language—hopefully out of harm's way. I'm too restless to stay here, so I think I will go on to the mountain cabin tonight. Stay safe, Boom! I'm not his only target you know."

"Yeah! Looks like we could have us a war, D.R. There is just one thing bothering me about Goren. He's smart, but no hero—certainly a math brain but not one to plan so well, unless he's learned a lot since I knew him. Think about who else could be working with him—a tactician, maybe a warrior like us. If I come up with anyone, I'll call. Take a few days to get your direction, then we'll go to work. Some people have been asking around for Marge, showed her picture around Forsyth. Naturally it got back to me. I figure it had to be Barfus. I'm carrying a gun at all times. I know you will do the same. Rest up. We'll be in touch."

Jacob watched them all drive away, including Annabelle. The cabin, which had always been his sanctuary, now seemed a lonely place. He felt edgy, anxious and wanted to be free — free in this case meant driving, looking at the countryside, stopping when he wanted to — and to see that view from the mountain cabin that Boom had described so vividly. Annabelle would join him later after her calls and a television interview. Then he would decide what to do about Barfus and Goren.

Chapter 22

Turning the last bend in the path, Little Lion saw his quarry. Jacob's brown Aussie hat, held secure by a strap under his chin, was pulled low over his eyes. His camouflage poncho billowed and sailed in the mist-laden wind as the roiling black clouds swept past, almost touching his head. He was a lonely sentinel, perched on this ancient outcrop of stone, awaiting the return of his soul.

Some change, either in the light or within his tense and alert mind, caused him to turn at Little Lion's silent arrival. In that instant, Little Lion saw the pain and torment reflected in Jacob Reynolds' face.

"My apologies for the interruption. There is a man to see you, Mr. Reynolds. He shows a government badge and his eyes are sincere. He is familiar?"

Jacob nodded, breaking his silent commune with the elements. He walked away from the precipice, stepping off the stone to follow Little Lion down the path back to the cabin.

Lion had been right. The man waiting had a good, strong face and stern but kind eyes that did look familiar. His build stated he was a man of action, held far too long in the confines of an office, judging from the small paunch at his belt line. Jacob grinned at Billy Joe Brown.

He walked up holding out his hand. "You don't look like any of the agents I've dealt with before, but that schnozzle certainly is familiar. What brings you to my neck of the woods?"

"The Company has reconsidered your resume and

George sent me down to offer you a job."

"You don't usually do it this way, do you Billy Joe?"

"No! There is a reason for this change in policy. Once you hear me out, you'll understand."

"How did you find me?"

"If you remember, I once gave you Bulldozer's address. He told me where to find you. George got Annabelle's information and knows you will find Goren Thomas. He prefers that you do so for us. We don't know where to tell you to start. Maybe you know more about this than we do. I came because an hour before we found the information on Goren Thomas and Martin Long the funds disappeared from all the banks, whisked overseas, then to God knows where. I want you on board and will be your main contact. As you know, drug money is like a cabalistic mistress — powerful, sexy and so irresistible few can refuse her charms. She is quite the most versatile of whores but never faithful."

"Sounds like you and George have a real problem in the whorehouse."

"You know damned well we do or I wouldn't be here. When you bring Goren in we will get all our questions answered. I'm sure you remember him as well as I do."

"Yeah, and obviously he never forgot me! But I never thought he was that smart. Billy, George knows I will get Goren, whether I work for the Company or not, and when I do get him he may no longer be able to talk."

"That's what's worrying George. He also thought it would be better if you got him *legally* and understood the reason we need him to talk. This is a blackout and if you decide to come with us, you will only have two contacts: myself and an agent known as Jerry Langston. You will only meet Jerry if something happens to me or we get in a tight and need him. Naturally, I hope you never meet him, but we both know the extent of the evil we face. We'll be working with no backup and little equipment. Bulldozer and Irish have agreed to work with us on an as-needed basis. I have access to satellite tracking through the Navy, but any electronic equipment we need, Johnny Irish will have to supply for us. Are you in? It's better than being a renegade getting in our way. Besides you will be paid to hunt the man you want so much, and until we get it straightened out you can no longer practice law."

"Subtle blackmail, huh?"

Billy grinned. "If necessary I'll get on my knees and beg. This sucker has compromised the agency and we need him and you're the best man for that job."

"You've convinced me. What do I need to do to set the game in motion?"

"Just sign these papers. George will hold them in his personal safe until this job is done. Here is your identification; we anticipated you would join us. We will deposit cash until other means can be worked out to put money into the construction company account. Don't worry about the IRS any longer — that is settled. Only use your ID under extreme circumstances. I figure I don't have to explain that. Here is all the latest information on Goren. We don't know where he is but suspect he has returned to this country. Probably he's traveling through drug channels." Billy Joe eased his tired six-foot-four frame out of the chair and walked to the window. "All local and major papers are carrying the story of your innocence and release from prison. That should goad Goren into looking for you. I understand this is the second time you've busted up his playhouse."

Jacob walked to the bar and poured them two bourbons straight, as Lion brought in a platter of sandwiches, sweets and a pot of coffee. "So you have set me up to be the mouse?"

"I would never make that mistake, D.R.. We both know you are not mouse material. You set yourself up with Goren the first time you routed his game. We just decided that we both had the same enemy. I'll be around should you need me but don't count on that. They may catch onto me . . . I used to be one of the best, but am only here now because we can't trust anyone else. I haven't been in the field in fifteen years." He handed D.R. what looked like a thin beeper. "This is an electronic calling card, but it only calls me or Jerry Langston. If you get in a tight, push Jerry's button, then mine. I can get here faster and he will need a few minutes. The blue one is mine and the red one is Jerry's. Don't go anywhere without it—clip it on your belt."

He walked over and held out his hand. "If you think of anything else you want to ask, call me at this number. In this box is a cell phone. It is secure, so call me only on that phone. I'm damned glad you'll be working with us. We sure as hell need your expertise. Just don't trust anyone—remember, only George, Jerry or myself and don't call George. If anything happens to me, call Jerry immediately." He walked to the table, took a plate and filled it with sandwiches, poured himself a cup of coffee and sat down, placing the plate on the coffee table.

"Damn, you're in better shape than I am. You don't look to have an ounce of fat on you. Worked out in prison huh?"

"Best way to exercise and I knew what I intended to do when I got out."

"It figures."

"I'll be flying back to DC tonight, but I will be back on Wednesday. Between now and then, should you need anyone call on Jerry. Otherwise, just forget about me. After Wednesday I'll be around and I will call you if I learn anything more. Keep that phone on you even when you sleep. Think Lion could pack me some of those sandwiches to eat on the road? They're damned good!"

"That will please him beyond words, Billy Joe."

After Billy Joe left, lunch sack in hand, D.R. stood looking at his new Agency ID, with not a little pride. Then he called Little Lion. "I need a slight adjustment to my utilities. Can your wife sew?"

"No problem, I will do it myself."

Jacob picked up the phone and called the warehouse. "I'll be back tomorrow afternoon around five. How about dinner and a drink somewhere, that is, if you and Zelda are free."

"As free as a couple with five kids can be. Damn! I'm glad you're out. Now we can get some work done. We'll be waiting at the warehouse. By the way, your wife, or I should say ex-wife, called. She said to tell you she's sorry she doubted you." D.R. didn't have an answer to that statement. "Will Annabelle be joining us?"

"No, she's flying to Washington tomorrow morning. Won't be back until Friday. I'll see you between five and six tomorrow afternoon. See you then!"

Waiting for Annabelle to get back from Atlanta, he sat in the rocker on the porch enjoying the view and thinking. Barfus sure had bad company eating with him from the rotten apple, and he was sure the attorney had no idea how bad. For all his intelligence in the courts, he had no training for men such as Goren could call on. He wondered where Barfus was hiding. Eventually they would find him and if he was after Marge to hurt her, it would be Boom. There was no doubt in his mind that Goren would be coming after him, or sending others to do the job. He would be a very visible 'mouse'.

The next morning a helicopter picked Annabelle up to fly her to the airport. Jacob was amazed at how good she made him feel. She was fantastic in bed, yet vulnerable and thoughtful and he thought, loyal. And that was important, since his wife had not been loyal.

That afternoon, driving down the mountain, Jacob recalled the action concerning Goren Thomas, now certain he was the man called Martin Long. Gore, as he had known Goren in Vietnam, had been in supply. The only problem was, he had supplied drugs — cocaine and heroin — that put two platoons on dirt naps. Working on the natural fear of men in war, he had promised heightened awareness to keep them ahead of the enemy, when in reality he was signing their death warrants. The bastard knew at the time what he was doing. Vividly, Jacob recalled looking under the tarp at the inside of the truck bed, the bodies of a platoon so mangled together one couldn't be distinguished from the other, bronzed together in one solid horror sculpture. The big howitzer hooked to the back of the truck, still intact. The guys had been stoned when attacked; they had not had a chance. The blame rested on Gore's shoulders.

What Jacob didn't know was that when he had ruined Gore's little drug kingdom, the man had returned to the States and gone full scale with college kids, working with the poppy kings, then with the cartels. He was too high to be touched now and his money was scattered everywhere.

Jacob remembered Gore as a good accountant, but not smart enough to run a global operation. Was he wrong about the man? Had he been the man driving the truck on the freeway over two years ago? The body posture was the same but the face different. Maybe he'd had a cosmetic restructure.

Billy Joe had said that Goren probably knew of Jacob's release and about the warrants for Barfus and himself within minutes after they were issued. An hour before his accounts were found he had transferred all monies to an account in Zurich and then to God knew where. They were still working on it. All they had were old copies of transactions.

Gore had been on vacation in Spain, when he had been informed of the Hull woman's treacherous confession and decided that they had only a month to live — and that long only because he had other fish to fry at the moment and that was also a job he wanted to do himself. Two hundred and forty-nine miles from where Jacob was driving, Gore was thinking that so far he was ahead of the Agency and he wanted to stay that way. When the money reached Spain, he had withdrawn it, caching it at a villa he owned under yet another name. The Agency could trace the money to Spain, but no further; by that time he would be back in Atlanta.

"Reynolds has done it to me again!" he raged, knocking over furniture and slamming his fist against the wall. "I'm going to kill the bastard and all of his friends! This time I will do it personally." A voice behind him said, "Dream on, little man, you couldn't kill D.R. if he were unarmed and you had a Uzi. Better confine yourself to the women. They're more your speed, but you can come along for the ride and watch the fun if you like."

"I told you when we were in Con Thien that we needed to kill that bastard. But no! You said you needed him. Now look what he's done to us again. I think you have a case on him!"

"Watch yourself, asshole, I'm running this show. Just because you are front man, don't get high-handed with me. Just look what we've built! We have a direct line into every government agency. How can that worn-out warrior cause us problems? Relax, enjoy your vacation and leave the work to real men. By this time next week he will be old news and that DA of his too.

Gore looked into those steely eyes and shivered inside. He had worked with the man for years but still feared him.

"I'm our gold card. D.R. will be looking for you, never expecting me."

Chapter 23

Following in the wake of a thunderstorm, Jacob tuned in to the sky-copter report. Traffic was a solid mass back to the Canton exit, so he took the off ramp at Shilo to Old Highway 41, then cut through on Stanley to Salem, then to Calvary and headed east on Georgia Highway 120. He cut through side streets to Cobb Parkway then turned South on I-285. It took a little longer but he wasn't sitting in traffic. Glancing at his watch as he pulled into the RBI parking lot, he was surprised to see it was 4:40 p.m. He was early.

Zelda's new dusty pink Buick Century was parked beside the steps and the door to the building was standing open, something they had a policy never to do. He pulled the Rover into the shade just inside the fence, walked in shadow to the side of the building, climbed up on the loading dock and opened the side door to the last bay. He hesitated before entering, closing his eyes to adjust his sight to the dim interior.

Sliding in the door, he quickly moved away from the entrance and waited. He could neither see nor hear anyone in the bays or the sleeping area; the place seemed deserted. Moving silently around equipment in the huge bays, he climbed the steps to the office door, which was also standing open. He heard a groan. Gun held high, he eased through the door to the construction office. Then in shock, he lowered the Glock and slid it into a shoulder holster. He ran to kneel beside Zelda, gently feeling for a pulse. It was there, but faint. He grabbed the phone and called 911, then got a wet cloth and gently cleaned her face. She had been badly beaten. He gently probed for broken bones, finding that both her arms were broken. He didn't move her, just rinsed the cloth and continued bathing her face. She moaned and opened her eyes. "Jacob . . . had to tell . . . they wanted Marge . . . stupid . . . they knew about the boys . . . were going to kill them all . . . big man hit me in the face and stomach . . . another man told him he had killed me. They left . . . so sorry, help Marge. . ."

"Zelda, you had no choice. Boom can handle himself."

"No! Seven or eight of them. Too many . . ."

Jacob dialed Boom's number, but there was no answer. He called Bulldozer's mobile and got him immediately. "Where are you, Dozer?"

"On my way back, I got halfway to Roswell and called. When there was no answer, I started back. I'm about a mile from I-285. Where do you all want to eat and I'll meet you and Zelda there."

"Dozer, I have something to tell you and I don't want you to wreck. Some scum broke in the office and beat Zelda—badly. The ambulance is just arriving. I'm sending her to the trauma center at Grady. It's the best! They beat her to find out where Marge is—said they were going to kill your boys if she didn't tell them and they knew exactly where the boys were. So, you see she had to tell them. Dozer, they broke both her arms, hit her in the stomach and broke her nose and blacked her eyes. I don't know how long ago it happened, but the blood is just coagulating so I must not be far behind them. I cleaned her face and she woke up and told me what happened. The MT's coming in now. She may have a broken pelvis. They're giving her oxygen and working on her, getting her ready to go. I can't go with her; I have to go after the bastards. I called for the ambulance, then tried to get Boom but there's no answer. Then I called you. You can swing by Grady; I'm calling Irish to meet the ambulance. She's going to make it, Dozer." Silently he prayed to God that she would. It's all my fault, Dozer, God! I'm sorry."

"Shut up, D.R. Get off the pity party and get your ass on the road to Boom's. Don't kill all the bastards — save a few for me, especially the one who beat Zelda. I'll be there soon as I can. Now move your ass, D.R. If even one of them gets away, I'll hold you responsible!" There was an angry sob in the big man's voice.

"I'm on my way. I'll keep phoning Boom. I'm thinking they may be out riding and forgot to take a phone. It has to be Barfus. Goren has no need of Marge."

"Okay, get both hands on the wheel and burn rubber. I'll meet you at Boom's just as soon as I can."

"Who took the message sending you to Gainesville?"

"I'll find out, you had better believe it."

"Okay! I'm out on this end."

Traffic was not heavy and he made good time driving as fast as the Rover would go. When he turned in at the gate, he could see it had been forced open. Knowing the long drive to the house, he quickly took the turns. Slowing just before the last turn to the house he took to the woods. Stopping the Rover, he hit the ground running straight for the front door, past the two vehicles parked there. The engines were still popping so he was right behind them.

He walked right in the front door. Looking past the potted palm, he could see Boom on the floor against the wall, holding his side. Blood seeped from between his fingers. A big black man was holding Marge by her hair with one arm twisted up behind her back. Barfus was playing with a shotgun, first ramming it against her belly, then under her chin. He moved it toward the floor as D.R. threw the knife that went right into Barfus' wrist, cutting the tendon. Barfus dropped the gun.

Bullets screamed past D.R., but apparently the men had not seen him. Reflected in a mirror he had seen the big man drop Marge and reach for the shotgun. In the interim, Marge ran into the library and slammed and locked the door. Two shotgun blasts told him they had opened that door, but he heard hard heels hitting pavement. In the distance a helicopter motor sputtered and then was silent. Marge had gone through the French doors and was running all out for the stables.

"Go catch her, Joey. Bring her back here. We're going to have some fun. Watch out for the knife thrower. It was probably one of the gooks that you said lived here." He would have said more, but the boy was flying down the path.

Joey caught Marge halfway to the barn, spun her around, caught her by the hair then twisted her arm behind her, forcing her ahead of him back up the path.

"Joey?" Joey turned to look at the person who had called his name, and met a fist. D.R. didn't think Marge needed to see more blood. But Joey wouldn't be going anywhere soon.

"Oh, God! D.R.! They've shot Boom. We've got to help him!"

"I know, but it's you Barfus wants. Go to the barn, get a horse and ride! Go to the Duncans."

"No! I don't want to leave Boom. I'll hide in the barn."

"All right, but don't come out until one of us comes after you. Go!"

Mitchell heard a noise and turned to see Joey sliding across the marble floor. "What the . . ." Mitchell was speechless at the sight of Joey crumpled on the floor.

Joey's brother checked him out. "He's dead. Don't see any blood—just a bruise on his temple."

"Get him out of the way . . . over there by the steps."

Armond Barfus was whining, holding his arm over the small bar sink. Sloe was trying to remove the knife and Benny was holding Barfus. Sloe pulled the knife out and Barfus fainted. They put a tourniquet on his arm, wrapped ice in a towel and wound it around the wounded arm.

"What do we do now, Uncle Marshall?"

"Keep that son-of-a-bitch alive; he knows where the money is. Now, we make a deal."

"I don't know who you are out there," he yelled. "I'll give you one minute to show yourself, or I'll kill this guy.

He's already got one of my bullets in him, but this one will kill him."

Jacob had no choice but to show himself. He just walked in and stood in the dining room door, his gun in the shoulder holster under his jacket.

"You talking to me?" he said and walked on into the room. Five guns turned toward him. "Barfus? This your crew? They look a little different from the company you usually keep. What the hell's going on? What are you all doing here?"

"I'm immune to your insults, Jacob. I figured the heroics had to be you. Where's Marge?"

"Not my heroics, and I have no idea where Marge is. I just got here and heard you yelling. What's the matter with your arm?"

"You know damned well what you did."

"Not me. I just told you! I just got here."

All the men looked at each other. "Then who did Joey?"

"Who is Joey?"

"That one over there."

"Are you okay, Boom?"

"I've had worse days."

Jacob stood where he was in the middle of the floor. He wanted to go to his friend and help him.

"Let me get some towels for him!"

"Ain't no need for that, you all gonna die."

"Who the hell are you guys and what do you want? Appears to me you're in the wrong stomping ground." They seemed amazed by his casual manner.

"We work for him," Benny said, pointing to the colonel.

"Shut up, Benny! Who we work for ain't none of his business."

"Oh! I see, the colonel thinks Marge caused all of his problems," D.R. said. "He doesn't understand that he did it himself and just got caught. You guys should know that you are making a big mistake. You see, that woman you beat up — and left for dead — is the wife of a fellow named Bulldozer. Bulldozer's best friend is Tony Brown. Ever heard of him? He's black like you with green eyes . . . remember — one of the most decorated blacks in the service? Now if you all are smart you'll leave old Barfus there for Bulldozer and light out. You've already done more damage than is allowed."

"Allowed? Allowed by whom? The police? Man . . . the police are just the clean-up squad!" It was Sloe talking.

"You guys are young to die, but it is your decision."

There was a wild mad look in Barfus' eyes. Red half-moons circled the folds of skin under his eyes and his clothes were wrinkled. Jacob supposed that dodging the police was more than he could handle. His pants were coated with blood and his arm, although the bleeding now seemed to be stopping, had soaked the towel he held so tightly with ice rolled up in it. He appeared close to blacking out again.

Tony could have saved those boys' lives had he been here. Maybe they would have listened to him. He could see they were high on something. Evidently Marshall provided drugs for them.

"Jacob, I have a job for you. You go find Marge and bring her back. I'll give you ten minutes, then I shoot your friend over there," Barfus demanded.

"You're crazy, man. He'll run straight to the cops! Benny, you and Sloe go get her. She's probably hiding in the barn. Don't do any funning, just bring her back up here."

"How you doing, Boom?" D.R. asked.

"A little like the slug Chew took — same place." He was telling D.R. that it hit a muscle and he couldn't get up. D.R. walked to the bar, picked up a clean towel and walked over to Boom. He stooped down and handed the towel to him. Inside he had slid a small slim gun he carried behind the waistband of his trousers. Boom took the towel and pressed it against his side. Looking over Jacob's head, he tried to flash a warning with his eyes, but too late as a gun barrel slammed D.R.'s skull.

The static in his brain reminded D.R. to wake up or die. He could hear heavy confusion all around, and he forced his eyes open a slit to see two of Marshall's men who had gone for Marge trying to stand in the doorway. Then they fell face first to the marble floor. Marshall was standing with his back to D.R., momentarily stunned to see his men out cold, so D.R. rolled over, hitting him hard behind the knees. Marshall tumbled backward over him, hitting the floor hard and losing his hold on the shotgun, which skidded toward the door to the dining room. They each dived for it and both grabbed the gun, holding it up between them. Strong as D.R. was, he was no match for Marshall. He tried to get to the trigger to discharge the shot into the ceiling but the big man kneed him in the stomach. Holding on, D.R. stepped back and kicked him in the knee and they both went down spinning around on the slick floor. The gun went off, pellets flying right into Marshall's men who were out cold on the floor.

"You damned idiot," D.R. mumbled through clenched teeth, "you just killed your own men."

Marshall kneed him in the crotch and slammed him hard with one huge fist, sending D.R. sliding across the floor. Marshall grabbed the gun and started to bring it up to fire. A hand came from nowhere and clipped his wrist, catching the gun as it flew from his grasp. Bulldozer set the safety and threw the gun to D.R.. "Damn, Dozer he just shot two of his own men."

"Yeah, I saw. Poor guys. The other three are gone too." He never took his eyes off Marshall. "What's your name man?"

"Marshall. You don't look like no bulldozer to me."

"D.R., look behind you. The old man is trying for that gun." D.R. snatched the Uzi and handed it to Boom, who handed him back his gun. "Come on, Barfus, here's you a ringside seat." Boom patted the floor beside him.

"D.R., catch!" Bulldozer threw him a remote phone. Dialing 911 for an ambulance, he saw Barfus heading for the window. He put one shot into the frame. "Don't even think about it. Bulldozer will want to talk with you next."

Dozer motioned to Marshall to come out, to fight him. Marshall, seeing that the man was unarmed, grinned through the sweat pouring down his face. "You want to fight me?"

"Yeah! Let's see if you can do as well with a man as you do beating up on women."

Bulldozer was just slightly smaller than the big boxer and at least fifty pounds lighter, but all of Dozer's weight was muscle. Marshall cautiously circled the man, waiting for him to make a move, waiting to get a good opening. He slid his hand in his pocket and flipped open a knife.

Boom leaned forward. "Move out of the way, D.R.. Before I bleed to death, I want to see this. Is Marge safe?"

"She was when I arrived," Bulldozer answered.

Marshall couldn't believe his luck; the man was walking right into his reach. He rammed a stab at Dozer's chest, then looked surprised as his knife went sliding across the floor. He had not even seen the man move. He hesitated only a moment, then sent a right to Dozer's head — a blow he envisioned going right through the man's skull. Bulldozer stepped aside, catching Marshall's wrist and twisting him into a flying mare. Marshall hit hard, skidding across the marble floor, stopping just before ramming the wall with his head.

Quick as a cat, Marshall jumped to his feet facing his adversary, thinking this might take a little longer than he thought. He waited, bending his knees slightly, adjusting his weight, moving a half step at a time while watching the man. Damn, he had not even seen that move. The man was fast!

He was watching for that fast right when a left punch bruised his ribs as the right came across in a cheek-splitting *splatt*. Before he could recover, the left slammed into his eye and another right split his nose, sending him stumbling backward.

Marshall had fought tough men and the sudden realization came to him that this one was not a boxer; this

man was a killer! What the hell had Barfus gotten him
into? The realization stunned him. He looked in those
brown eyes — tiger eyes — and saw for the first time in his
life a man who knew him, a man who was merely toying
with him; to this man he was simply a mouse, and, Good
God! He had beat up the man's wife. This was one fight
he had to win, or die. Seeing an opening, he swung a
powerful right to the body and the man only grunted,
stepped back, fell to the floor and kicked him in the balls.
Marshall doubled over and a knee split skin above his
right eye. Marshall remembered he had used his fist on
the woman's mound and had also busted her nose.
Through the pain, the survival instinct pushed him on.
He slowly got to his feet, hardly able to breathe.

The shrill of a siren could be heard in the distance.
Marshall decided to head ram the bastard. Picking his
chance, he charged, head down. Turning in a half squat,
Bulldozer let the man's momentum drive him forward, then
grabbed his arm, putting him off balance. He brought up
his knee in a chop just below the man's heart. He heard the
man's ribs break inward and knew he would be dead in a
few minutes. He watched as the man slowly slid to the
floor. He looked at Boom and said, "I didn't want to get
any more blood on your floor."

"I appreciate that, Dozer. Mine will be enough to clean
up."

Bulldozer then turned to Barfus, but spoke to D.R., "I
know you have a prior deed to this man, but he ordered
Marshall to beat Zelda. Want to flip for him?"

"Naw! He only manipulated to disbar me; that's
insignificant in comparison to what he did to Zelda. What's
the report from the hospital?"

"She's in surgery; Mary and Johnny are with her. Well,
what do you say . . . I've got to get out of here before that
ambulance arrives."

"How did you get here so fast?"

"I flew the bank's goddamned chopper."

"You! Flew? A helicopter?"

"Hell! I always could. Chew insisted I learn—said I might need to know how sometime. I just don't want all that I can do known—it's safer to have an edge."

"Well, I'll be damned! You can have Barfus . . . I can stand the pain of loss."

"No, Jacob, don't give me to that animal," Barfus begged. "I'll confess to everything—just call the police."

Bulldozer walked up to Barfus. "I am the police. Do you think for one minute I would turn you over to some slick lawyers." He turned to Jacob. "No slight intended, friend."

"None taken."

"We're going for a little ride. Don't worry, I won't kill you—but the fall might. Get Marge out of the barn on your way out, D.R."

"See you at Grady."

Pushing Barfus in front of him, Bulldozer took him out the back door as the ambulance came to a screeching halt at the front.

Chapter 24

The early risers straggled down the wide curved stairway to the sitting room, following the faint, wisping aroma of freshly brewed coffee. Zelda, stretched out in the fully extended recliner, was wrapped in a soft butter-yellow blanket. She snuggled infant Johnny Leland Michaels in the hollow created by her casts, nuzzling his fuzzy red hair. The bruises outlining her eyes shone silver and purple in the flickering light. The huge old stone fireplace before her was radiating warmth as light from gas-fed flames curled around large artificial logs. Bulldozer was stretched out on the carpet in front of the fire at her feet, the handle of a gun protruding from the shoulder holster under his left arm, a war bag close at hand. In a sleepy stupor they sat watching the flames dance in the fireplace while sipping their coffee, simply enjoying the quiet, the warmth and the companionship of close friends.

Other than the wind chill factor of eighteen degrees, it was a beautiful sunny day. Mary and Johnny had been at Boom's place all week, along with Irish, installing a better alarm system. "You know, Zelda, Mun Sun and his wife have been wonderful with the babies. They have spoiled me rotten."

Mary sat in an overstuffed chair holding the other twin. "I talked with Lili when they got back home from her niece's wedding. At first I was suspicious of them being gone at that particular time of danger—legal thinking I suppose— until I found out that preparations for the wedding had been going on for over a year. Anyone could have known they would not be here. The time picked, I suppose was a random thing."

Bulldozer snorted, "I don't believe in random."

"Good morning, ladies and little gentlemen." D.R. came in, taking off a heavy parka. He bowed to the ladies and babies. "Are you all the only early risers?"

"No, my youngest three boys are in the game room. The other two are sleeping off a late night there."

"Zelda! Will you please remember that I had something to do with bringing those boys into the world. Maybe you could say *our* boys," Dozer said.

"Oh! Bulldozer! All you did was have all the fun; I did the suffering!"

"Listen to the woman. You'd think she was the only one who lost sleep, walked the babies to sleep all by herself. Why I was the fastest diaper changer in town."

"That's true, darling, you couldn't stand the odor."

"What a picture that makes. Bulldozer changing a diaper with that gun sticking out of the shoulder holster and a war bag beside the diapers." Mary grinned at him. He made a face at her.

"Pour me a mug of coffee, will you Jacob. Use that mug with the long straw. Two sugars and two dollops of cream."

"Dollops? Yeah! I can do dollops."

"And three teaspoons of sugar, it's a big mug."

"I can handle that! You look very pretty for a lady who took on a professional boxer and six goons. But those bruises show you need a little retraining, or maybe we should just get you a gun belt with a six-shooter and tie it down to your leg when you get well. You know, like the cowboys wore and you can practice a fast draw while riding Boom's big black stallion."

"I don't want a six-gun. If it ever happens again, I want an Uzi!"

Jacob was glad to see she still had spunk — that being a victim had not made her one. Some unexpected happenings in life can make any of us victims, but only if we allow it to fester. Zelda's had been exceptionally brutal and he knew how close it had been. Had he not gotten back early . . . He shuddered, realizing that both Mary and Zelda were alive because he had been on the scene at the right time. He had not been the reason for Mary's problems but he felt responsible for Zelda's.

Bulldozer and Zelda and their five boys had arrived the night before, Zelda, straight out of the hospital and still unable to walk or sit straight, recovering from a fractured pelvis, broken ribs, broken arms and operations. The severe internal tears from the beating necessitated a hysterectomy. Sarah was there nursing Zelda, and Boom, who was recovering from his gunshot wound to the side, and Jacob from his wounds.

Walking across to the fireplace, Jacob said, "This looks like a damned field hospital!" He squatted on his heels beside Bulldozer. "We have three wounded in this new war, Dozer. I'm going to do my best to make sure there are no more. I have to take Annabelle back early in the morning. She has a court case at ten. I've asked her to have her men around her at all times and she will. I'm going back to the cabin late tomorrow afternoon after we find the snitch. If Goren is going to hit both places, he will have to divide his forces, and I don't think he will. He'll hit me first I'm thinking, then if successful, he'll come for the rest of you. I intend to see that he doesn't get this far."

"Then he won't," Dozer said, "but we both know he may hit here first. I've been thinking it might be better to send the family away. But that would only put a different set of innocents in target range. It would be easier clean-up here without publicity like the last time. I ran it by Billy and he agrees, but because of the leaks at the department, he can't promise any help beforehand."

D.R. nodded and stood, making a show of stirring the fire. "Of course, you all know that I was out at daybreak cutting those logs to keep you warm," he said, grinning.

"Yeah!" Irish said as he walked in. "You even sump-pumped the gas to go under the logs, didn't you?" Irish put his big hands on D.R.'s shoulders and shook him. "Thanks, Buddy!"

"Yeah, and I ground those little coffee beans with my teeth. Oh, well, all my secrets are out. Can you believe this plantation? The smokehouse doesn't smoke, the fireplaces are gas fired, there are no shuck mattresses on the beds, and the kitchen and bathrooms are inside. Ah! But Miss Scarlett is here!" They all turned to see Marge appear in the doorway wrapped in a beautiful green silk robe.

"Miss Scarlett never had it so good," Marge said, entering the room, smiling like a contented cat. She gave Jacob a hug and kiss on the cheek, then did the same to everyone in the room.

"My jobs are done, having lit the fire and made the coffee. Rhett Reynolds will now view his vast holdings from the bay window," Jacob said.

Outside, the day was clear and the sun was shining, but he knew the wind had a bite to it that chilled to the bone, for he had already been out on horseback for a reconnaissance ride around the estate.

In the pasture, horses turned their tails to the wind and continued to nibble the rich winter grass. Some huddled for warmth. "Boom! You may want to get the horses in the barn. It's pretty damned cold out there," D.R. said, coming back inside.

"How cold do you think it is?"

"I'd say the wind chill factor is about ten."

Boom looked out the window and then picked up a phone. "Hey! Bradley! We need to get the horses in the barn." He listened to the boy's suggestion and then said, "That's fine, put the stallions in the corner stalls, the rest in the middle. Yeah! It's okay to turn on the big heaters, but keep the temperature at around fifty-five degrees. Their combined body heat will run it higher." Boom pushed the off button on the phone and turned back to D.R.. "Thanks, D.R. I've been lazy this morning, didn't realize how cold it was getting."

"Yeah! The man takes a bullet, has major muscles re-stitched and is recuperating and he says he's lazy? Boom, you never knew a lazy day."

"Until now. D.R., now I have lazy days. You noticed the workmen finished repairing the plaster in the dome and entry. The library door was shredded beyond repair, but Harvey managed to find a suitable replacement. Irish said he gave you a tour of our terrorist room with a separate communications system, something I should have done years ago. It was easy because the older part of this house had one already from Civil War days. Sometimes you don't realize you need an escape hatch until it is too late."

Boom was still weak but healing, his arm in a sling to keep him from moving it and pulling the stitches in his side and back open. But even he was armed to the gills. An Uzi in a hastily constructed bag hung beside him, and a Glock was stuck down in the cushion at his side, extra clips lined up beside it.

"Mary, you and Irish had better take advantage of us and sleep all you can. There will be little rest in the coming years. With five boys, I speak from experience," Zelda said, smiling.

Marge looked at Boom and said, "Are you listening, Boom? See what you're getting yourself into?" Everyone stopped stupefied, looking from Marge to Boom and back again. Zelda squealed, "Marge! You're pregnant!"

"Yes! I just found out yesterday. The baby is due around the sixth of May."

"Boom, I can't believe it—after all these years." D.R. gave him a high five. "Congratulations! I'm pretty damned jealous you know."

Boom looked a little sheepish. "I guess we'll have to have one of those shotgun weddings, with me holding the shotgun. I've been trying to talk her into marrying me for a long time."

Bulldozer was off the floor now, dancing a jig. "I sure hope it's a girl. My boys need women!"

Irish was pouring champagne in glasses at the small

bar. "Okay! Let's toast the future generations!"

"Listen up, you guys! I've been saving this edition for a time like this," D.R. said. "This is from two weeks ago. The reporter suggested that any would-be robbers take note: The house you target to rob just may be owned by a former Green Beret."

D.R., Boom, Bulldozer, Irish and Jason looked at one another and said, "Former?"

"There was an article last week in the Journal. Yeah! Here it is. Well known attorney, Armond Barfus, is believed to have left the country to evade prosecution on charges of brutal rape of a minor, etcetera, etcetera . . ."

Bulldozer spoke quietly in an aside to Boom and D.R., "Well now, I wouldn't exactly say that he skipped the country . . . I would say that he is probably in charge of a fair parcel of swampland."

Chapter 25

Marge turned with concern to their still convalescing friend. "Zelda, are you warm enough?" Zelda was wrapped in blankets, holding the baby close to her cheek.

"Hmmm . . . nothing smells so wonderful as a clean baby. I'm nice and warm, thank you, Marge. The doctor thinks I'll be able to sit up soon, but five sons will have to be enough. I lost a few parts in the rampage. We had always hoped for a daughter, but now it'll be up to the boys to give us granddaughters. I'm just grateful to be alive."

Marge picked up little redheaded Matthew Michaels from Zelda's arms. "Johnny Leland and Matthew Reynolds Michaels, fine names for two fine looking boys."

Watching Zelda, D.R. was amazed at her good humor, and only taking aspirin for the pain. Jacob thought of the men who were responsible for that pain. God! Some men were such animals that not even a good woman could civilize them. He walked to the bar and poured a couple of fingers of Compari in a tall glass, then smoothed it out with about an equal dose of Vodka. This stuff smelled and tasted like jet fuel.

He was staying in today, resting. Annabelle had worn him out last night and she was sleeping in this morning. Guess he wore her out too. Somewhere out there was Goren and he would be along soon, but today Jacob would rest and let the others keep watch. He walked back to the window. Out in the pasture, Bradley was rounding up the horses. Jacob smiled. The boy rode well. He had on a cowboy hat and was obviously having a good time.

Irish sidled up alongside. "You're going after Goren, aren't you?"

"I won't have to go after him. He'll find me."

"Damn, D.R., you can't do it alone. And Dozer and I can't leave Mary and the babies or Zelda and the boys. Goren has threatened to kill them as well."

"I have some help from our other source, so don't worry."

Irish was torn, but he had to protect the women and children, there was no other option. He also knew that alone D.R. would be a sitting duck!

"None of us will ever forget that Goren's drug game caused two platoons to be wiped out—maybe more than that. We know how much *mercy* he can muster. The only place you and Dozer can be is here!"

Irish dropped his head. "None of us will ever forget that, D.R. Dammit! I don't need reminding."

"What happened, D.R.?" Mary sat up, hearing the anguish in Johnny's voice. She leaned forward.

Sarah stood up and walked over to put her arms around D.R. "I'm not sure you should hear that, Mary. It's pretty grim stuff. It's one of the many reasons Bob shot himself."

Mary saw the warning look Irish was giving D.R. "I need to know, Johnny! Anything that brings that kind of anguish to your eyes will only help me to understand what you have experienced. Also, I need to understand . . . for the boys."

Irish gave D.R. the okay sign. "All right, Mary, but just remember you asked. Maybe it is best that you all know the type of man we're facing. Back during the war, Gore was in supply, only he supplied the ground troops with cocaine, heroin, any drugs they wanted. He told the guys that the drugs would keep them safer, because drugs heightened awareness. The guys were so stoned that they didn't know where they were when they drove right into an enemy convoy, took a direct hit. When I looked under the tarp into the truck all I could see was a melded black mass of bodies so glued together that one could not be distinguished from another. Goren heightened their awareness all right, sent them to heaven straight through hell! Bob was supposed to be with them, but he had been nipped by a sniper the week before and was laid up. He always thought, since he was not on drugs, that if he had been there he could have saved them. We tried to tell him he was not the driver and would have died also but there were other factors in the war that got to him. Bob could never adjust to the indifference."

Bulldozer walked over to put an arm around Sarah and picked up the story. "Sarah was his nurse. They married over there and she tried everything to bring him around. Nothing worked. His demons finally caught up with him."

Boom rolled his wheelchair closer to the group. "I've invited Sarah and Jason to move into the caretaker's house. They'll be staying here with us until I get it renovated. We're adding rooms and refurbishing in case you two want to start a family."

"I have enough babies to look after, Boom — you included!"

Boom smiled at the affectionate barb and said, "I am spread pretty thin these days and Jason has agreed to help me out. Beyond that house toward town is approximately fifteen hundred acres of nice rolling land with springs and one lake. I'm hoping you guys will want to build a house there. Jason is going to help do lot layouts, water and sewage plans and cut roads into the property. I don't want Marge and the baby to be so isolated. The three thousand acres on the other side will remain a part of the plantation. We'll talk more about this after our little problem is solved."

Bulldozer put his hand on D.R.'s shoulder. "Goren was recently located in Spain but by the time an agent got there, he had already left for parts unknown. They did get fingerprints and they are Goren's, but the picture on that passport as Martin Long does not match the Goren we knew. He must have had plastic surgery. We could have been seeing him around town for years without knowing his true identity."

"How tall was he, Dozer? About five-six?"

"Yeah, good accountant and very smart with the computers."

"He must have been the one who tried to kill me on the freeway."

"I have a little sailboat, D.R. She's well stocked and has a Vietnamese crew. I charter her out of Savannah to business enterprises—legitimate ones. My captain is Bob Wrenn. Remember him?"

Bulldozer looked at him hard, "Hell! Man. When we move we don't have time to sail."

Boom laughed. "Don't think it will take as long as you might assume. Wait until you see her."

Bulldozer grinned. "I should have known. What's her name?"

"The Longlegger."

"I should have expected that too. When did you rename her?"

"Oh! About two years ago."

Jacob turned his back to the fire and smiled at the group. "I have a better suggestion. Why don't we take the women on a cruise when this is all over, go to the islands. Maybe I can talk Annabelle into taking a vacation. I seldom get to see her. She's working all the time and so tired that she is sleeping in this morning."

"Get her pregnant, then she'll stay home," Irish suggested.

"Good idea, Irish. I've been trying, but maybe not hard enough."

"You men! You never stop." Sarah picked up an empty glass, filled it with Champagne and handed it to Zelda.

"Sounds good to me! I think my injuries could stand feeling the hot sand on my back and sea breezes ruffling my hair."

"And me beside you on the beach," Bulldozer added as he kissed her, his eyes flickering up as Sun walked in.

"You guys want some breakfast?   It's on the buffet. I left you a little." He grinned.

Their conversation came to a halt when they heard: "Reggie! Bring me a plate of ham and eggs and grits, I'm hungry!"

"They all turned to look at Bulldozer Bush, saying in unison, "Reggie?"

"Oh, hell, Zelda! Now you've done it! They'll never let me live that one down. My real name is Reginald Allen Bush the fourth. But if anyone but Zelda ever calls me Reggie, I'll bust his nose!"

"Irish, Boom and D.R. grinned then snorted laughter as they hurried to the dining room.

After breakfast, Bulldozer pulled D.R. aside. "There's something about Goren's operation that's still nagging at me. He was an expert with computers but not a field man and definitely not warrior material. Someone is helping him, someone with our expertise, and he probably has a network of associates since he's had years to build up his distribution system. You be extra watchful when you leave. I know he will not sit still and wait for you. He's a sneaky bastard, but smart as all get out. Don't underestimate him. By breaking up his party twice, you are number one on his list and we all want to make damn sure he doesn't get you."

"Dozer, Goren's mine!"

"Sure, I owe you that and you can have him. All I'm saying is that he will not be alone, and whoever is helping him is no slouch. Now that I think seriously about what I've heard, Goren could not possibly have that kind of muscle power or expertise unless it's hired. You know our grapevine. I would've heard if there was any hiring being done of our kind of guys."

"It's for sure he's already here," D.R. said, putting his cup down on the hearth. "I didn't think he knew about the new babies, but he does! Billy Joe picked up one of Goren's men on another charge and he talked. Goren wants to kill us all—the women, the children . . . the man has no conscience."

"Granted he has a large organization in place, but he can't jeopardize it for personal revenge. So he will come after you himself, along with maybe a few men. He still thinks eliminating us will solve his problem, he doesn't know about our friend. We still have a problem with a sneak. Someone at the warehouse is Goren's man. He knows where to find us all, and we have no idea where to start looking for him."

"Bulldozer, I think I know how to find out just who the ferret is and let him lead us to Goren. First thing tomorrow you call Arnold and tell him that I'm staying home this week—that I fell down my back steps or something."

"You think he's the sneak?"

"Not at all, just tell him to tell the other guys at the morning meeting. I'll be out and around and will take it from there. Have plenty of sandwich meat and fixings in the refrigerator. None of the men will go out to lunch and buy food if it's there for free, unless there is another reason."

On Monday, Arnold, working over some sewage grading plans, pulled up his sleeve and looked at his watch. It was almost noon. Following Bulldozer's advice, he had given Jacob's message to the men at the morning briefing. Arnold had not gone out to lunch; he had fixed a *Dagwood* sandwich and was eating while studying the drawings for the groundwork on the new project when Bulldozer called. "Are all the other guys back from lunch yet?"

"I'll check with Lee and call you back."

Five minutes later Arnold called back. "All of the guys stayed but Andy Smith. He said he wanted a pizza; he should be back soon. Oh, and Bobby Staten had to take his mother to the doctor. He'll be in later. That was planned last week."

"Arnold, will you pull Andy's file and let me know where he stands insurance-wise. I'm not sure we brought him up to date. I'll hold the phone."

"Dozer, everything looks in line. He has one sister and she's listed as beneficiary. All the forms look to be in order and sent in the day he came to work."

"Good work, Arnold. I'm as close as the phone. Zelda is having a little difficulty so I'm staying here with her for a few days. I'm depending on you to keep the work going."

"I'll handle it. Tell Zelda I hope she feels better soon."

Returning the file, Arnold went back to work, a curious expression on his face, for he knew his boss never asked a question without a reason.

Cold and tired, Jacob only wanted two things: a hot bath and a cup of scalding black coffee. But when he drove up the driveway, he saw an old blue jeep parked in front of the cabin. A man sat on the hood, drinking from a thermos. He was wearing utilities and a pair of scruffy lace-up boots. He also had on a heavy, fleece-lined jacket with a rumpled soft brimmed hat pulled down to his ears. A war bag rested on the hood beside him.

One of the old school, D.R. thought as he pulled his Rover behind the car and turned off the ignition. He had been in the woods all morning beside the warehouse and wanted a bath. Andy Smith had told him all he knew, which was only that Goren was in town along with the phone number he had just called to tell Goren that Reynolds was at home. Jacob had fired Andy and let him go, only to have him turn on him with a knife. That had been Andy's last mistake.

As he got out of the truck, D.R. adjusted the silenced special built .22 in his pocket. The small caliber was efficient if the shooter was experienced. The man removed his crumpled hat and D.R. recognized Billy Joe.

"D.R., we have a problem. Goren is in town."

"Yeah! I know. You need to go. Word is out to lure him here. He had a spy in my business. His name was Andy Smith — *was*. We set him up and he bought the bait. All he could tell me was that Goren was here; he didn't know where, but he gave me the phone number that he had called. I fired him and let him go, Billy, then he turned on me with a knife. You know how I hate for someone to come at me with a knife."

"That's one less to contend with, D.R."

D.R. nodded, but it didn't make it any easier.

"He had told Goren where to find me, which was the plan. I picked him up as he returned around one o'clock and we talked for a couple of hours. So Goren has had plenty of time to get here."

"Is that coffee hot?"

"Yeah! Got a cup?"

"Yeah in the car, just a minute."

D.R. took the thermos and poured his cup full and took a tentative sip. "Ahh! Man you make good coffee."

"D.R., I'm not leaving. Where can I park my car?"

"Billy, don't get into this. This is my personal war. You leave, and leave now!"

Billy Joe was fiddling with a small electronic unit, sweeping it over the woods. "Too late for me to leave, we've got company. At least twelve to fifteen men moving through the woods up on the ridge."

"Shit! That many? Goren was faster than I thought."

Gulping the rest of the coffee as he took the steps to the house four at a time, D.R. said, "Come on!" Unlocking the door, he ran to his room and grabbed his war bag, calling to Billy Joe, "This way!" He lifted a trap door and hurried down the rough wood steps with Billy Joe right behind him. "Pull it closed behind you and lock it! Come on. Through here."

"You got enough firepower in that war bag or do you need anything?"

"Got all I need," he yelled as he followed D.R. through the well-shored tunnel. They came up under an overhanging rock about fifty yards southeast of the cabin.

"Stay here, Billy Joe. Unless they stick their heads through the brush they won't see you. I won't get between you and the house, so shoot anything that moves." He hoped Stark was out somewhere hunting; he wouldn't allow himself to think that the dog may have been killed.

Billy pulled out a Smith & Wesson nine millimeter with a silencer. D.R. nodded. "Excellent! You can stay here and quietly pick them off. It'll take them time to locate you. If they do get your direction, drop down in the tunnel and find another outlet—there are three. I'm going to meet them. Sorry to get you into this Billy—stay alive!"

Billy would never admit that he felt trapped, but he was on unfamiliar terrain and unlike D.R., wasn't in the best of shape. If he lived through this he would get himself in as good a shape as possible for a fifty-five year old paper pusher.

It wasn't the odds that worried D.R.. He didn't want to lose Goren under any circumstances. He had to stay alive, no matter what, to get Goren.

Billy Joe unbuttoned an inner pocket, pulled out a small phone and punched the redial button.

D.R. immediately slipped out of the tunnel and into the surrounding brush. Taking a page from Bulldozer's book, he found a hidey-hole and waited. They came down the ridge behind the house so fast that he didn't have long to wait. He pushed a switch on a remote and lights went on in the bedroom of the house. Someone to his right said, "He's there. You guys go to the right of the house. You know what to do. Let's get this over with quick. Now move!" The man talking put a pair of binoculars to his eyes and bought eternity.

D.R. cleaned his knife, took the man's monitor, earphone and binoculars and waited. He heard movement to his left and the monitor vibrated, "We're in place." A sharp voice spoke, "Move in!" At that news, D.R. felt a fury rage inside. This was going to be a Bloody Monday. He took the hat from the man he had killed and put it on his head. He poked his head through the evergreens where he had heard the voice. When the man turned he hesitated, seeing the hat, and lost his life.

Two down, how many to go? He stretched both men out and crossed their arms over their chests, Bulldozer style. If any of the enemy had been in Vietnam, that should scare the shit out of them. He moved back up the ridge, waiting, knowing he had the advantage. Listening to the monitor, he heard a man calling number one. "Boss, you need to see this. Four and six are down in area three."

"On my way."

When Number One got to area three, he found three men in a row with arms crossed over their chests. He gasped, "It can't be. We just called twenty minutes ago and he answered the phone."

D.R. pushed his remote and the bedroom light went out and one came on in the den. "Someone's in the house," a man said. "Move down. Get close then rake the house."

Another man stumbled over him and D.R. took him out. He borrowed the man's nine-millimeter Glock, checked the load. He moved down behind the others keeping an eye on Number One, who was moving beyond some pines behind his advancing men. D.R. looked to the right and when he returned his gaze to the moving men, Number One was gone.

When they started shooting up the cabin he took four of them out. Seven down, how many to go? He moved back up the ridge. Number One was slick; he had smelled a trap and had gotten away. That voice was familiar. It wasn't Goren, but who the hell was it?

D.R. found a spot and waited, listening intently. He pushed a button and turned all the lights off inside the cabin. Then he turned on an outside spotlight on the east end of the house. He saw three men jump back into the surrounding woods, but not before Billy put a bullet into one. That amounts to seven down one injured, but how many were there in all?

The monitor vibrated and he listened, "Regroup, sector four. Group two, move in sector five."

Okay! D.R. knew that sector three was directly behind the house, sector four was east of the house, and sector five must be west. Sectors one and two were in front. From his hiding place he watched for activity west of the house, and wasn't disappointed. He saw bushes moving and heard slight scuffling. Now he had four to his right and how many to his left? He listened and didn't hear anything. He waited for one of them to come close. They didn't. He heard the door burst open and gunfire in the house. Damn them, he would have to repair that mess! Then the lights came on and the monitor vibrated again. "Nothing here, the damned place is empty. There's a government car out front."

"Get out of there. I'm coming down."

D.R. did not see or hear any movement. It was a trap to try to smoke him out. He waited. The men came out of the house and started back west. Suddenly he heard the unmistakable sound of an SVD. The men coming out of the house started hollering and running and shooting back into the woods below the house. They fell like ducks in a shooting gallery by whoever held the Russian Dragunov. This man was brutal, noisy and efficient. Dozer and Irish were just as deadly, but they were always quiet. Had Billy called Jerry?

He started to move then felt the cold steel of a gun against the back of his head.

"Drop the gun, and turn slowly. I want you to see your executioner."

When D.R. hesitated, the man reiterated, "I said turn around you damned bastard. You wiped out my entire platoon, now you're going to die a piece at a time. I said drop the weapon!"

D.R. complied, dropping the Glock to the forest mulch. Did the man believe he could possibly move that fast? That he could get from beyond those men to here in that span of time. Slowly D.R. turned and in the light from the spotlight on the house he recognized his adversary.

The crewcut was the same. The man was in good shape for his age, except for his eyes, which were wild with fury. "Sherman? My God! I thought you were dead! Damn, you were the best of us all! Goren turned you? I don't believe this!"

"Turned me? You fucking asshole, I run Goren! That asshole has no nerve, only brains. You should never have bucked us. But it didn't matter — we did better here in the states. Now, you've done it again . . . for the last time. I'm going to take you apart piece by fucking piece like cutting up a chicken."

Behind the blazing eyes, D.R. saw the drug-induced frenzy and decided to take a chance. Sherman had stepped back to allow him to turn around. The man was furious, wanting to kill D.R., but first he wanted to play with him. When the fist suddenly flashed out, D.R. was ready. In one smooth movement he ducked the fist, grabbed Sherman's gun hand and threw his weight into the man. Sherman had been too sure of himself. The gun went flying into the underbrush, as D.R. rolled and came up with his knife in his hand. So did Sherman. "Dammit! Sherman! We've been through the same stuff, suffered the same injustices!"

"Yes! It has been great getting back at them, stuffing their stupid kids with drugs . . . breaking up those stuffy families who looked down their noses at us. Teaching them a lesson they will never forget! Now it's your turn."

"I don't want to kill you, Sherman. I'll get you some help. You should never have gone after those kids; they were stupid — stupid just like we were when we went to war. You were wrong to do that, Sherman, dead wrong. You fucked up everything the rest of us stood for. Don't make me kill you!"

"The day wasn't born that you could kill me, D.R. What kind of help do you want to give me? Stick me in some hole in a hospital and fill me with drugs to keep me quiet? Out of sight and out of mind?"

D.R. knew what the man said was true, that actually none of them were playing with a full deck. Some just held better cards to begin with that kept them in check.

"D.R., you've been a thorn in my side for twenty-five

years. Take it like a man or just take it."

With no excess of motion, Sherman pulled a long thin knife from his sleeve, tilted the tip on his finger where a tiny ooze of blood formed. He quickly grasped the blade and in a blur of motion began the throw. Then suddenly he stiffened and the knife dropped from his hand as he stood there in surprise. A small dark hole appeared above his nose.

D.R. watched the man fall. He leaned over and picked up the Glock. He knew Sherman would have killed him, because he just could not kill his former friend and mentor, who had been listed as missing in action twenty-five years ago.

"It's Billy Joe, D.R., don't shoot! This man behind me is Jerry Langston." He motioned to the man holding the black SKS Russian rifle in his hand, along with a small caliber silenced pistol in the other. Jerry nodded in D.R.'s direction.

"We think Goren is on the ridge. Jerry spotted three men waiting with their vehicles when he came in that way."

"All right, we go—but Goren is mine, understand."

"Only if it works out that way, D.R.. No lives will be lost unnecessarily to fulfill your revenge." It was Jerry speaking. D.R. thought he looked capable. He was at least six foot three or so and all lean muscle, probably about thirty-six years old. No Vietnam vet, that one. He had taken Sherman out with a Ruger .22 caliber with silencer. Sherman, he knew, had met a far easier death than he deserved.

"I can handle that, Jerry. Now if you gentlemen will follow me, I know the easiest and quickest way to the top."

They hunched down, watching the men at the trucks. One straggler came out of the woods opposite yelling, "It was a fucking trap! They're all down, all gone but me!"

It was the man Billy had wounded. Blood seeped through his shirt and he was holding his right arm in a tight grip against his body.

A man stepped down from a pickup truck and said,

"Even Sherman?"

The face was different but the voice was the same. It was Goren.

"I don't know. I didn't see him. Everyone was down and I never did see anyone, like ghosts they were! Fire coming from everywhere and didn't see anybody!"

"You fucking bastard! You left Sherman to die? My best friend!" Goren was screaming now. He pulled out a .38 and shot the man standing in surprise before him. Turning to the two shocked men behind him, he said, "Load up! Let's get out of here."

As they started for the vehicles, D.R. put a bullet in the ground in front of Goren. "Hey Goren! We got your boyfriend. Now it's your turn." He kept shooting, getting the man farther away from the vehicles. Jerry added his part to panicking the three men, putting bullets right under their noses.

"Government Agents! Throw down your weapons and you will not be hurt. You are under arrest."

The two men with Goren started to put up their hands and Goren brought his gun around to shoot his own men. Jerry shot Goren's gun hand and the other two quickly held up their hands. Goren dodged for the woods.

"There he goes, D.R.! He's all yours. Bring him back alive! Alive I say, so we can get the rest."

D.R. slipped away before Goren was out of sight. He moved through familiar terrain, knowing exactly the path the man would take. The line of least resistance through the woods was a path leading to an old logging road that wound down the ridge. D.R. followed a deer trail down the other side, found a hiding place beside the logging road and waited for Goren. He knew that on top of the ridge Jerry and Billy would be cuffing the men and calling for clean-up.

D.R. let Goren go past then stepped onto the road behind him. "You won't make it, Goren. Your number's up. Sorry I don't have a truck to put you in so I could throw in a round or two of shells."

Goren stopped. Slowly he turned around. D.R. knew the man had a gun. He walked closer, and with his left fist, hit him in the jaw. Goren fell, rolled and then got shakily to his feet. In his other hand he held the .38. With one easy movement, D.R. slipped a thin-bladed knife from his utilities. He threw the knife in one fluid motion and the blade went to the hilt in Goren's wrist. He dropped the gun, horror registering on his face seeing the knife protruding from either side of his wrist.

D.R. screamed, "You fucker! You've never felt pain before, have you? You always had Sherman to protect you. Want to know how he died? A bullet between the eyes! You corrupt little bastard; you destroy everything you touch . . ."

D.R. looked at the man sitting in the dirt holding his wrist, babbling like a baby. A multi-millionaire; backer of politicians; instigator of his disbarment. He heard movement behind him. He spun around, gun ready.

It was Jerry. "We need him, D.R. He'll be more useful to us alive. He will tell us all about his organization and that takes precedence over any other action."

"No! His lawyers will only buy him out. You don't know, Jerry. He has caused so much death."

"D.R., we'll keep him in solitary until we're through with him. Believe me, we need his operation more than you need revenge. Then he will go to a maximum-security prison. He is guilty of murdering the man on the ridge, in addition to his other crimes."

While Jerry was talking, he moved to Goren's side. He grabbed the man's wrist and pulled the knife out slowly, slicing the tendon as he did, making it deliberately painful as the man screamed, then fainted. "He's a pathetic piece of shit, D.R. He's not worthy of being killed by you. He'll get his in prison." He wrapped a handkerchief around the man's wrist and tied it tightly. Then he cleaned the knife in the dirt and handed it back to D.R..

"You did an excellent job. It's a pleasure to work with a professional like you. Man, you move quietly in the woods. I'd like to work out with you sometime and learn how to move like you do. I didn't see you at any time, but I saw and heard Sherman."

At the sound of choppers, Jerry looked up. "I hear the clean-up crew. Let's get this piece of trash to transport. They'll send a carpenter crew in a couple of hours to repair the damage. Maybe we can find a pot without a hole in it to make some coffee and light a fire in the fireplace. I don't remember it ever being so damn cold in the field."

Jerry gave Goren a shot to put him to sleep and threw him over his shoulder. "It's almost over, buddy. Just as soon as Billy gets some *medicine* down Goren, we'll have the whole story."

D.R. pulled out a folding phone, turned it on and dialed the plantation. "Yeah! Bulldozer here."

"It went down a few minutes ago. There were fourteen men, Goren and a man we thought dead—Sherman. You were right, he had superior muscle and intelligence all right, and he had Sherman. Sherman was running Goren."

D.R. knew that Dozer was as stunned as he had been.

"You talking about missing-in-action Sherman?"

"Yeah! One and the same."

"You kill Sherman?"

"No! I couldn't do it! He knew his sudden reappearance would shock me, and took advantage of that fact. When the bullet hit him, the knife was in his hand and moving to take me out. It was that close. He had a much easier death than a lot that we both remember. I don't understand how he could've lived all this time without a whisper in the ranks."

"What about Goren? Did he come out unscathed?" Bulldozer's voice was hard. Jacob knew Dozer was disappointed that he had missed the fight. As he talked with Dozer on the phone, D.R. and Jerry were walking down to the cabin.

"Goren is injured. His right hand will be useless from now on, but he will live to sleep and tell. Our friend says to tell you it's over. We'll talk with you later. Where's my girl?"

"On her way there . . . alone. Warn the guys so no one accidentally shoots her."

"Okay! I'm out on this end."

D.R. folded the phone and turned to Jerry. "Let your men know that a woman is on the way in and to let her through."

"Okay, will do."

"Jerry, I don't mind telling you, I was shocked speechless at seeing Sherman. He would've killed me because I would not have shot him. He taught me everything I learned over there. I went in as a FAC and he was in the next hole. He was a trusted friend. Those first few weeks, he saved my life several times. I was trained, but green to the killing. When he went missing, it hurt, and I took it out on a lot of the enemy. Thanks, Jerry, for saving my life."

They had reached the cabin and were going up the steps. "You think I did, D.R., but you didn't realize you were already moving. It's an automatic response when faced with death. He would've hurt you, that's for sure, but not where he had aimed. You would've killed him in a split second. I saw it all. I just didn't see any reason to let you get hurt in the process. You see, psychologically you would've had to be hurt first in order for your psyche to accept killing someone you admired, someone you considered a friend at your back. Anyway, you're welcome. See what you can find to brew us some coffee while I light the fire. It's all over now."

"I don't accept that, Jerry."

"Why not, D.R.? Sherman said he was running Goren."

"Did you see Sherman's eyes, Jerry? He was on something. Nobody on drugs could handle that kind of an operation, and Goren was just a bean counter trying to be a warrior. He was smart, but he didn't have the capacity to run and control this kind of a field operation. There had to be someone else running the show."

D.R. turned to look directly at Jerry. "Who the hell are you, Jerry? You didn't waste a shot out there . . ."

The screeching of tires interrupted them and they both hit the floor.

Annabelle came running up the steps, hands in the air, her yellow cashmere coat flying out behind her. Jerry looked at D.R. and laughed. "I didn't spill a drop of coffee, did you?"

"Not a drop!"

They both laughed as Annabelle threw herself in Jacob's arms.

"Jacob! Jacob! Are you hurt?" She was running her hands all over him, checking for blood.

"No . . . no bullet holes . . . but don't stop. Keep checking . . . just a little lower . . . I think I might have a scratch on my . . ."